The Lovely Lady

The
Lovely Lady

D. H. Lawrence

Fredonia Books
Amsterdam, The Netherlands

The Lovely Lady

by
D. H. Lawrence

ISBN: 1-58963-963-4

Reprinted from the 1933 edition

Fredonia Books
Amsterdam, The Netherlands
http://www.fredoniabooks.com

Contents

Contents

The Lovely Lady

At seventy-two, Pauline Attenborough could still sometimes be mistaken, in the half-light, for thirty. She really was a wonderfully preserved woman, of perfect *chic*. Of course, it helps a great deal to have the right frame. She would be an exquisite skeleton, and her skull would be an exquisite skull, like that of some Etruscan woman, with feminine charm still in the swerve of the bone and the pretty naïve teeth.

Mrs. Attenborough's face was of the perfect oval and slightly flat type that wears best. There is no flesh to sag. Her nose rode serenely, in its finely bridged curve. Only her big grey eyes were a tiny bit prominent on the surface of her face, and they gave her away most. The bluish lids were heavy, as if they ached sometimes with the strain of keeping the eyes beneath them arch and bright; and at the corners of the eyes were fine little wrinkles which would slacken with haggardness, then be pulled up tense again, to that bright, gay look, like a Leonardo woman who really could laugh outright.

Her niece Cecilia was perhaps the only person in the world who was aware of the invisible little wire

3

which connected Pauline's eye-wrinkles with Pauline's will power. Only Cecilia *consciously* watched the eyes go haggard and old and tired, and remain so, for hours; until Robert came home. Then, ping! —the mysterious little wire that worked between Pauline's will and her face went taut; the weary, haggard, prominent eyes suddenly began to gleam; the eyelids arched; the queer curved eyebrows, which floated in such frail arches on Pauline's forehead, began to gather a mocking significance, and you had the *real* lovely lady, in all her charm.

She really had the secret of everlasting youth; that is to say, she could don her youth again like an eagle. But she was sparing of it. She was wise enough not to try being young for too many people. Her son Robert, in the evenings, and Sir Wilfred Knipe sometimes in the afternoon to tea; then occasional visitors on Sunday, when Robert was home; for these she was her lovely and changeless self, that age could not wither, nor custom stale; so bright and kindly and yet subtly mocking, like Mona Lisa who knew a thing or two. But Pauline knew more, so she needn't be smug at all, she could laugh that lovely mocking Bacchante laugh of hers, which was at the same time never malicious, always good-naturedly tolerant, both of virtues and vices. The former, of course, taking much more tolerating. So she suggested, roguishly.

Only with her niece Cecilia she did not trouble to keep up the glamour. Ciss was not very observant, anyhow; and more than that, she was plain; more still, she was in love with Robert; and most of all, she was thirty, and dependent on her Aunt Pauline. Oh, Cecilia! Why make music for her!

Cecilia, called by her aunt and by her cousin Robert just Ciss, like a cat spitting, was a big dark-complexioned pug-faced young woman who very rarely spoke, and, when she did, couldn't get it out. She was the daughter of a poor Congregational minister who had been, while he lived, brother to Ronald, Aunt Pauline's husband. Ronald and the Congregational minister were both well dead, and Aunt Pauline had had charge of Ciss for the last five years.

They lived all together in a quite exquisite though rather small Queen Anne house some twenty-five miles out of town, secluded in a little dale, and surrounded by small but very quaint and pleasant grounds. It was an ideal place and an ideal life for Aunt Pauline, at the age of seventy-two. When the kingfishers flashed up the little stream in the garden, going under the alders, something still flashed in her heart. She was that kind of woman.

Robert, who was two years older than Ciss, went every day to town, to his chambers in one of the Inns. He was a barrister, and, to his secret but very deep mortification, he earned about a hundred pounds a year. He simply *couldn't* get above that figure, though it was rather easy to get below it. Of course, it didn't matter. Pauline had money. But then what was Pauline's was Pauline's, and, though she could give almost lavishly, still, one was always aware of

5

having a *lovely* and *undeserved* present made to one: presents are so much nicer when they are undeserved, Aunt Pauline would say.

Robert too was plain, and almost speechless. He was medium-sized, rather broad and stout, though not fat. Only his creamy, clean-shaven face was rather fat, and sometimes suggestive of an Italian priest, in its silence and its secrecy. But he had grey eyes like his mother but very shy and uneasy, not bold like hers. Perhaps Ciss was the only person who fathomed his awful shyness and *malaise*, his habitual feeling that he was in the wrong place: almost like a soul that has got into the wrong body. But he never did anything about it. He went up to his chambers, and read law. It was, however, all the weird old processes that interested him. He had, unknown to everybody but his mother, a quite extraordinary collection of old Mexican legal documents, reports of processes and trials, pleas, accusations, the weird and awful mixture of ecclesiastical law and common law in seventeenth-century Mexico. He had started a study in this direction through coming across a report of a trial of two English sailors, for murder, in Mexico in 1620, and he had gone on, when the next document was an accusation against a Don Miguel Estrada for seducing one of the nuns of the Sacred Heart Convent in Oaxaca in 1680.

Pauline and her son Robert had wonderful evenings with these old papers. The lovely lady knew a little Spanish. She even looked a trifle Spanish herself, with a high comb and a marvellous dark brown shawl embroidered in thick silvery silk embroidery. So she would sit at the perfect old table, soft as velvet in its deep brown surface, a high comb in her hair, ear-rings with dropping pendants in her ears, her arms bare and still beautiful, a few strings of pearls round her throat, a puce velvet dress on, and this or another beautiful shawl, and by candlelight she looked, yes, a Spanish high-bred beauty of thirty-two or three. She set the candles to give her face just the chiaroscuro she knew suited her; her high chair that rose behind her face was done in old green brocade, against which her face emerged like a Christmas rose.

They were always three at table; and they always drank a bottle of champagne: Pauline two glasses, Ciss two glasses, Robert the rest. The lovely lady sparkled and was radiant. Ciss, her black hair bobbed, her broad shoulders in a very nice and becoming dress that Aunt Pauline had helped her to make, stared from her aunt to her cousin and back again, with rather confused, mute, hazel eyes, and played the part of an audience suitably impressed. She *was* impressed, somewhere, all the time. And even rendered speechless by Pauline's brilliancy, even after five years. But at the bottom of her consciousness were the data of as weird a document as Robert ever studied: all the things she knew about her aunt and cousin.

Robert was always a gentleman, with an old-fashioned punctilious courtesy that covered his shyness quite completely. He was, and Ciss knew it, more confused than shy. He was worse than she was.

The Lovely Lady

Cecilia's own confusion dated from only five years back—Robert's must have started before he was born. In the lovely lady's womb he must have felt *very* confused.

He paid all his attention to his mother, drawn to her as a humble flower to the sun. And yet, priest-like, he was all the time aware, with the tail of his consciousness, that Ciss was there, and that she was a bit shut out of it, and that something wasn't right. He was aware of the third consciousness in the room. Whereas, to Pauline, her niece Cecilia was an appropriate part of her own setting, rather than a distinct consciousness.

Robert took coffee with his mother and Ciss in the warm drawing-room, where all the furniture was so lovely, all collectors' pieces—Mrs. Attenborough had made her own money, dealing privately in pictures and furniture and rare things from barbaric countries —and the three talked desultorily till about eight or half-past. It was very pleasant, very cosy, very homely even: Pauline made a real home cosiness out of so much elegant material. The chat was simple, and nearly always bright. Pauline was her *real* self, emanating a friendly mockery and an odd, ironic gaiety. Till there came a little pause.

At which Ciss always rose and said good-night and carried out the coffee tray, to prevent Burnett from intruding any more.

And then! Oh, then, the lovely glowing intimacy of the evening, between mother and son, when they

8

deciphered manuscripts and discussed points, Pauline with that eagerness of a girl, for which she was famous. And it was quite genuine. In some mysterious way she had *saved up* her power for being thrilled, in connexion with a man. Robert, solid, rather quiet and subdued, seemed like the elder of the two: almost like a priest with a young girl pupil. And that was rather how he felt.

Ciss had a flat for herself just across the courtyard, over the old coachhouse and stables. There were no horses. Robert kept his car in the coachhouse. Ciss had three very nice rooms up there, stretching along in a row one after another, and she had got used to the ticking of the stable clock.

But sometimes she did not go up to her rooms. In the summer she would sit on the lawn, and from the open window of the drawing-room upstairs she would hear Pauline's wonderful heart-searching laugh. And in the winter the young woman would put on a thick coat and walk slowly to the little balustraded bridge over the stream, and then look back at the three lighted windows of that drawing-room where mother and son were so happy together.

Ciss loved Robert, and she believed that Pauline intended the two of them to marry: when she was dead. But poor Robert, he was so convulsed with shyness already, with man or woman. What would he be when his mother was dead?—in a dozen more years. He would be just a shell, the shell of a man who had never lived.

9

The Lovely Lady

The strange unspoken sympathy of the young with one another, when they are overshadowed by the old, was one of the bonds between Robert and Ciss. But another bond, which Ciss did not know how to draw tight, was the bond of passion. Poor Robert was by nature a passionate man. His silence and his agonized, though hidden, shyness were both the result of a secret physical passionateness. And how Pauline could play on this! Ah, Ciss was not blind to the eyes which he fixed on his mother, eyes fascinated yet humiliated, full of shame. He was ashamed that he was not a man. And he did not love his mother. He was fascinated by her. Completely fascinated. And for the rest, paralyzed in a life-long confusion.

Ciss stayed in the garden till the lights leapt up in Pauline's bedroom—about ten o'clock. The lovely lady had retired. Robert would now stay another hour or so, alone. Then he too would retire. Ciss, in the dark outside, sometimes wished she could creep up to him and say: "Oh, Robert! It's all wrong!" But Aunt Pauline would hear. And anyhow, Ciss couldn't do it. She went off to her own rooms, once more, and so for ever.

In the morning, coffee was brought up on a tray to each of the three relatives. Ciss had to be at Sir Wilfred Knipe's at nine o'clock, to give two hours' lessons to his little granddaughter. It was her sole serious occupation, except that she played the piano for the love of it. Robert set off to town about nine. And, as a rule, Aunt Pauline appeared to lunch, though sometimes not until tea-time. When she appeared, she looked fresh and young. But she was inclined to fade rather quickly, like a flower without water, in the daytime. Her hour was the candle hour.

So she always rested in the afternoon. When the sun shone, if possible she took a sun bath. This was one of her secrets. Her lunch was very light, she could take her sun-and-air bath before noon or after, as it pleased her. Often it was in the afternoon, when the sun shone very warmly into a queer little yew-walled square just behind the stables. Here Ciss stretched out the lying-chair and rugs, and put the light parasol handy in the silent little enclosure of thick dark yew hedges beyond the red walls of the unused stables. And hither came the lovely lady with her book. Ciss then had to be on guard in one of her own rooms, should her aunt, who was very keen-eared, hear a footstep.

One afternoon it occurred to Cecilia that she herself might while away this rather long afternoon by taking a sun bath. She was growing restive. The thought of the flat roof of the stable buildings, to which she could climb from a loft at the end, started her on a new adventure. She often went on to the roof: she had to, to wind up the stable clock, which was a job she had assumed to herself. Now she took a rug, climbed out under the heavens, looked at the sky and the great elm-tops, looked at the sun, then took off her things and lay down perfectly serenely, in a corner of the roof under the parapet, full in the sun.

The Lovely Lady

It was rather lovely, to bask all one's length like this in warm sun and air. Yes, it was very lovely! It even seemed to melt some of the hard bitterness of her heart, some of that core of unspoken resentment which never dissolved. Luxuriously, she spread herself, so that the sun should touch her limbs fully, fully. If she had no other lover, she should have the sun! She rolled voluptuously. And suddenly, her heart stood still in her body, and her hair almost rose on end as a voice said very softly, musingly in her ear:

"No, Henry dear! It was not my fault you died instead of marrying that Claudia. No, darling. I was quite, quite willing for you to marry her, unsuitable though she was."

Cecilia sank down on her rug powerless and perspiring with dread. That awful voice, so soft, so musing, yet so unnatural. Not a human voice at all. Yet there must, there must be someone on the roof! Oh! how unspeakably awful!

She lifted her weak head and peeped across the sloping leads. Nobody! The chimneys were far too narrow to shelter anybody. There was nobody on the roof. Then it must be someone in the trees, in the elms. Either that, or terror unspeakable, a bodiless voice! She reared her head a little higher.

And as she did so, came the voice again:

"No, darling! I told you you would tire of her in six months. And you see, it was true, dear. It was true, true, true! I wanted to spare you that. So it wasn't I who made you feel weak and disabled, want-

ing that very silly Claudia; poor thing, she looked so
woebegone afterwards! Wanting her and not wanting
her, you got *yourself* into that perplexity, my dear. I
only warned you. What else could I do? And you
lost your spirit and died without ever knowing me
again. It was bitter, bitter ——"

The voice faded away. Cecilia subsided weakly on
to her rug, after the anguished tension of listening.
Oh, it was awful. The sun shone, the sky was blue, all
seemed so lovely and afternoony and summery. And
yet, oh, horror!—she was going to be forced to believe
in the supernatural! And she loathed the supernatural,
ghosts and voices and rappings and all the rest.

But that awful creepy bodiless voice, with its rusty
sort of whisper of an overtone! It had something so
fearfully familiar in it too! and yet was so utterly
uncanny. Poor Cecilia could only lie there unclothed,
and so all the more agonizingly helpless, inert, collapsed in sheer dread.

And then she heard the thing sigh! A deep sigh that
seemed weirdly familiar, yet was not human. "Ah,
well; ah, well, the heart must bleed! Better it should
bleed than break. It is grief, grief! But it wasn't my
fault, dear. And Robert could marry our poor dull
Ciss tomorrow, if he wanted her. But he doesn't care
about it, so why force him into anything!" The
sounds were very uneven, sometimes only a husky
sort of whisper. Listen! Listen!

Cecilia was about to give vent to loud and piercing
screams of hysteria, when the last two sentences

arrested her. All her caution and her cunning sprang alert. It was Aunt Pauline! It must be Aunt Pauline, practising ventriloquism or something like that! What a devil she was!

Where was she? She must be lying down there, right below where Cecilia herself was lying. And it was either some fiend's trick of ventriloquism, or else thought transference that conveyed itself like sound. The sounds were very uneven. Sometimes quite inaudible, sometimes only a brushing sort of noise. Ciss listened intently. No, it could not be ventriloquism. It was worse, some form of thought transference. Some horror of that sort. Cecilia still lay weak and inert, terrified to move, but she was growing calmer, with suspicion. It was some diabolic trick of that unnatural woman.

But *what a devil* of a woman! She even knew that she, Cecilia, had mentally accused her of killing her son Henry. Poor Henry was Robert's elder brother, twelve years older than Robert. He had died suddenly when he was twenty-two, after an awful struggle with himself, because he was passionately in love with a young and very good-looking actress, and his mother had humorously despised him for the attachment. So he had caught some sudden ordinary disease, but the poison had gone to his brain and killed him, before he ever regained consciousness. Ciss knew the few facts from her own father. And lately, she had been thinking that Pauline was going to kill Robert as she had killed Henry. It was clear murder: a mother murdering her sensitive sons, who were fascinated by her: the Circe!

"I suppose I may as well get up," murmured the dim unbreaking voice. "Too much sun is as bad as too little. Enough sun, enough love thrill, enough proper food, and not too much of any of them, and a woman might live for ever. I verily believe for ever. If she absorbs as much vitality as she expends! Or perhaps a trifle more!"

It was certainly Aunt Pauline! How, how horrible! She, Ciss, was hearing Aunt Pauline's thoughts. Oh, how ghastly! Aunt Pauline was sending out her thoughts in a sort of radio, and she, Ciss, had to *hear* what her aunt was thinking. How ghastly! How insufferable! One of them would surely have to die.

She twisted and she lay inert and crumpled, staring vacantly in front of her. Vacantly! Vacantly! And her eyes were staring almost into a hole. She was staring into it unseeing, a hole going down in the corner from the lead gutter. It meant nothing to her. Only it frightened her a little more.

When suddenly out of the hole came a sigh and a last whisper. "Ah, well! Pauline! Get up, it's enough for today!"—Good God! Out of the hole of the rain-pipe! The rain-pipe was acting as a speaking-tube! Impossible! No, quite possible. She had read of it even in some book. And Aunt Pauline, like the old and guilty woman she was, talked aloud to herself. That was it!

A sullen exultance sprang into Ciss's breast. *That*

was why she would never have anybody, not even Robert, in her bedroom. That was why she never dozed in a chair, never sat absent-minded anywhere, but went to her room, and kept to her room, except when she roused herself to be alert. When she slackened off, she talked to herself! She talked in a soft little crazy voice, to herself. But she was not crazy. It was only her thoughts murmuring themselves aloud.

So she had qualms about poor Henry! Well she might have! Ciss believed that Aunt Pauline had loved her big, handsome, brilliant first-born much more than she loved Robert, and that his death had been a terrible blow and a chagrin to her. Poor Robert had been only ten years old when Henry died. Since then he had been the substitute.

Ah, how awful!

But Aunt Pauline was a strange woman. She had left her husband when Henry was a small child, some years even before Robert was born. There was no quarrel. Sometimes she saw her husband again, quite amicably, but a little mockingly. And she even gave him money.

For Pauline earned all her own. Her father had been a Consul in the East and in Naples, and a devoted collector of beautiful and exotic things. When he died, soon after his grandson Henry was born, he left his collection of treasures to his daughter. And Pauline, who had really a passion and a genius for loveliness, whether in texture or form or colour, had laid the basis of her fortune on her father's collection. She had gone on collecting, buying where she could, and selling to collectors and to museums. She was one of the first to sell old, weird African wooden figures to the museums, and ivory carvings from New Guinea. She bought Renoir as soon as she saw his pictures. But not Rousseau. And all by herself, she made a fortune.

After her husband died, she had not married again. She was not even *known* to have had lovers. If she did have lovers, it was not among the men who admired her most and paid her devout and open attendance. To these she was a "friend."

Cecilia slipped on her clothes and caught up her rug, hastening carefully down the ladder to the loft. As she descended she heard the ringing musical call: "All right, Ciss!" which meant that the lovely lady was finished, and returning to the house. Even her voice was marvellously young and sonorous, beautifully balanced and self-possessed. So different from the little voice in which she talked to herself. *That* was much more the voice of an old woman.

Ciss hastened round to the yew enclosure, where lay the comfortable chaise-longue with the various delicate rugs. Everything Pauline had was choice, to the fine straw mat on the floor. The great yew walls were beginning to cast long shadows. Only in the corner, where the rugs tumbled their delicate colours, was there hot, still sunshine.

The rugs folded up, the chair lifted away, Cecilia

stooped to look at the mouth of the rain-pipe. There it was, in the corner, under a little hood of masonry and just projecting from the thick leaves of the creeper on the wall. If Pauline, lying there, turned her face towards the wall, she would speak into the very mouth of the hole. Cecilia was reassured. She had heard her aunt's thoughts indeed, but by no uncanny agency.

That evening, as if aware of something, Pauline was a little quicker than usual, though she looked her own serene, rather mysterious self. And after coffee she said to Robert and Ciss: "I'm so sleepy. The sun has made me so sleepy. I feel full of sunshine like a bee. I shall go to bed, if you don't mind. You two sit and have a talk."

Cecilia looked quickly at her cousin.

"Perhaps you would rather be alone," she said to him.

"No, no," he replied. "Do keep me company for a while, if it doesn't bore you."

The windows were open, the scent of the honeysuckle wafted in, with the sound of an owl. Robert smoked in silence. There was a sort of despair in the motionless, rather squat body. He looked like a caryatid bearing a weight.

"Do you remember Cousin Henry?" Cecilia asked him suddenly.

He looked up in surprise.

"Yes, very well," he said.

"What did he look like?" she said, glancing into her

cousin's big secret-troubled eyes, in which there was so much frustration.

"Oh, he was handsome; tall and fresh-coloured, with mother's soft brown hair." As a matter of fact, Pauline's hair was grey. "The ladies admired him very much; he was at all the dances."

"And what kind of character had he?"

"Oh, very good-natured and jolly. He liked to be amused. He was rather quick and clever, like mother, and very good company."

"And did he love your mother?"

"Very much. She loved him too—better than she does me, as a matter of fact. He was so much more nearly her idea of a man."

"Why was he more her idea of a man?"

"Tall—handsome—attractive, and very good company—and would, I believe, have been very successful at law. I'm afraid I am merely negative in all those respects."

Ciss looked at him attentively, with her slow-thinking hazel eyes. Under his impassive mask, she knew he suffered.

"Do you think you are so much more negative than he?" she said.

He did not lift his face. But after a few moments he replied:

"My life, certainly, is a negative affair."

She hesitated before she dared ask him:

"And do you mind?"

He did not answer her at all. Her heart sank.

The Lovely Lady

"You see, I am afraid my life is as negative as yours is," she said. "And I'm beginning to mind bitterly. I'm thirty."

She saw his creamy, well-bred hand tremble.

"I suppose," he said, without looking at her, "one will rebel when it is too late."

That was queer, from him.

"Robert," she said, "do you like me at all?"

She saw his dusky creamy face, so changeless in its folds, go pale.

"I am very fond of you," he murmured.

"Won't you kiss me? Nobody ever kisses me," she said pathetically.

He looked at her, his eyes strange with fear and a certain haughtiness. Then he rose and came softly over to her, and kissed her gently on the cheek.

"It's an awful shame, Ciss!" he said softly.

She caught his hand and pressed it to her breast.

"And sit with me sometime in the garden," she said, murmuring with difficulty. "Won't you?"

He looked at her anxiously and searchingly.

"What about mother?" he said.

Ciss smiled a funny little smile, and looked into his eyes. He suddenly flushed crimson, turning aside his face. It was a painful sight.

"I know," he said, "I am no lover of women."

He spoke with sarcastic stoicism against himself, but even she did not know the shame it was to him.

"You never try to be!" she said.

Again his eyes changed uncannily.

The Lovely Lady

"Does one have to try?" he said.

"Why, yes! One never does anything if one doesn't try."

He went pale again.

"Perhaps you are right," he said.

In a few minutes she left him, and went to her rooms. At least, she had tried to take off the everlasting lid from things.

The weather continued sunny, Pauline continued her sun baths, and Ciss lay on the roof eavesdropping in the literal sense of the word. But Pauline was not to be heard. No sound came up the pipe. She must be lying with her face away into the open. Ciss listened with all her might. She could just detect the faintest, faintest murmur away below, but no audible syllable.

And at night, under the stars, Cecilia sat and waited in silence, on the seat which kept in view the drawing-room windows and the side door into the garden. She saw the light go up in her aunt's room. She saw the lights at last go out in the drawing-room. And she waited. But he did not come. She stayed on in the darkness half the night, while the owl hooted. But she stayed alone.

Two days she heard nothing, her aunt's thoughts were not revealed, and at evening nothing happened. Then the second night, as she sat with heavy, helpless persistence in the garden, suddenly she started. He had come out. She rose and went softly over the grass to him.

"Don't speak," he murmured.

The Lovely Lady

And in silence, in the dark, they walked down the garden and over the little bridge to the paddock, where the hay, cut very late, was in cock. There they stood disconsolate under the stars.

"You see," he said, "how can I ask for love, if I don't feel any love in myself. You know I have a real regard for you ——"

"How can you feel any love, when you never feel anything?" she said.

"That is true," he replied.

And she waited for what next.

"And how can I marry?" he said. "I am a failure even at making money. I can't ask my mother for money."

She sighed deeply.

"Then don't bother yet about marrying," she said. "Only love me a little. Won't you?"

He gave a short laugh.

"It sounds so atrocious, to say it is hard to begin," he said.

She sighed again. He was so stiff to move.

"Shall we sit down a minute?" she said. And then as they sat on the hay, she added: "May I touch you? Do you mind?"

"Yes, I mind! But do as you wish," he replied, with that mixture of shyness and queer candour which made him a little ridiculous, as he knew quite well. But in his heart there was almost murder.

She touched his black, always tidy hair with her fingers.

22

The Lovely Lady

"I suppose I shall rebel one day," he said again, suddenly.

They sat some time, till it grew chilly. And he held her hand fast, but he never put his arms round her. At last she rose and went indoors, saying good-night.

The next day, as Cecilia lay stunned and angry on the roof, taking her sun bath, and becoming hot and fierce with sunshine, suddenly she started. A terror seized her in spite of herself. It was the voice.

"Caro, caro, tu non l'hai visto!" it was murmuring away, in a language Cecilia did not understand. She lay and writhed her limbs in the sun, listening intently to words she could not follow. Softly, whisperingly, with infinite caressiveness and yet with that subtle, insidious arrogance under its velvet, came the voice, murmuring in Italian: "Bravo, si, molto bravo, poverino, ma uomo come te non lo sara mai, mai, mai!" Oh, especially in Italian Cecilia heard the poisonous charm of the voice, so caressive, so soft and flexible, yet so utterly egoistic. She hated it with intensity as it sighed and whispered out of nowhere. Why, why should it be so delicate, so subtle and flexible and beautifully controlled, while she herself was so clumsy! Oh, poor Cecilia, she writhed in the afternoon sun, knowing her own clownish clumsiness and lack of suavity, in comparison.

"No, Robert dear, you will never be the man your father was, though you have some of his looks. He was a marvellous lover, soft as a flower yet piercing as a humming-bird. No, Robert dear, you will never

23

know how to serve a woman as Monsignor Mauro did. Cara, cara mia bellisima, ti ho aspettato come l'agonizzante aspetta la morte, morte deliziosa, quasi quasi troppo deliziosa per un' anima humana—Soft as a flower, yet probing like a humming-bird. He gave himself to a woman as he gave himself to God. Mauro! Mauro! How you loved me!"

The voice ceased in reverie, and Cecilia knew what she had guessed before, that Robert was not the son of her Uncle Ronald, but of some Italian.

"I am disappointed in you, Robert. There is no poignancy in you. Your father was a Jesuit, but he was the most perfect and poignant lover in the world. You are a Jesuit like a fish in a tank. And that Ciss of yours is the cat fishing for you. It is less edifying even than poor Henry."

Cecilia suddenly bent her mouth down to the tube, and said in a deep voice:

"Leave Robert alone! Don't kill him as well."

There was a dead silence, in the hot July afternoon that was lowering for thunder. Cecilia lay prostrate, her heart beating in great thumps. She was listening as if her whole soul were an ear. At last she caught the whisper:

"Did someone speak?"

She leaned again to the mouth of the tube.

"Don't kill Robert as you killed me," she said with slow enunciation, and a deep but small voice.

"Ah!" came the sharp little cry. "Who is that speaking?"

The Lovely Lady

"Henry!" said the deep voice.

There was dead silence. Poor Cecilia lay with all the use gone out of her. And there was dead silence. Till at last came the whisper:

"I didn't kill Henry. No, NO! Henry, surely you can't blame me! I loved you, dearest. I only wanted to help you."

"You killed me!" came the deep, artificial, accusing voice. "Now, let Robert live. Let him go! Let him marry!"

There was a pause.

"How very, very awful!" mused the whispering voice. "Is it possible, Henry, you are a spirit, and you condemn me?"

"Yes! I condemn you!"

Cecilia felt all her pent-up rage going down that rain-pipe. At the same time, she almost laughed. It was awful.

She lay and listened and listened. No sound! As if time had ceased, she lay inert in the weakening sun. The sky was yellowing. Quickly she dressed herself, went down, and out to the corner of the stables.

"Aunt Pauline!" she called discreetly. "Did you hear thunder?"

"Yes! I am going in. Don't wait," came a feeble voice.

Cecilia retired, and from the loft watched, spying, as the figure of the lovely lady, wrapped in a lovely wrap of old blue silk, went rather totteringly to the house.

25

The Lovely Lady

The sky gradually darkened, Cecilia hastened in with the rugs. Then the storm broke. Aunt Pauline did not appear to tea. She found the thunder trying. Robert also did not arrive till after tea, in the pouring rain. Cecilia went down the covered passage to her own house, and dressed carefully for dinner, putting some white columbines at her breast.

The drawing-room was lit with a softly shaded lamp. Robert, dressed, was waiting, listening to the rain. He too seemed strangely crackling and on edge. Cecilia came in, with the white flowers nodding at her breast. Robert was watching her curiously, a new look on his face. Cecilia went to the bookshelves near the door, and was peering for something, listening acutely. She heard a rustle, then the door softly opening. And as it opened, Ciss suddenly switched on the strong electric light by the door.

Her aunt, in a dress of black lace over ivory colour, stood in the doorway. Her face was made up, but haggard with a look of unspeakable irritability, as if years of suppressed exasperation and dislike of her fellow-men had suddenly crumpled her into an old witch.

"Oh, aunt!" cried Cecilia.

"Why, mother, you're a little old lady!" came the astounded voice of Robert; like an astonished boy; as if it were a joke.

"Have you only just found it out?" snapped the old woman venomously.

The Lovely Lady

"Yes! Why, I thought—" his voice trailed out in misgiving.

The haggard, old Pauline, in a frenzy of exasperation, said:

"Aren't we going down?"

She had never even noticed the excess of light, a thing she shunned. And she went downstairs almost tottering.

At table she sat with her face like a crumpled mask of unspeakable irritability. She looked old, very old, and like a witch. Robert and Cecilia fetched furtive glances at her. And Ciss, watching Robert, saw that he was so astonished and repelled by his mother's looks, that he was another man.

"What kind of a drive home did you have?" snapped Pauline, with an almost gibbering irritability.

"It rained, of course," he said.

"How clever of you to have found that out!" said his mother, with the grisly grin of malice that had succeeded her arch smirk.

"I don't understand," he said with quiet suavity.

"It's apparent," said his mother, rapidly and sloppily eating her food.

She rushed through the meal like a crazy dog, to the utter consternation of the servant. And the moment it was over, she darted in a queer, crab-like way upstairs. Robert and Cecilia followed her, thunderstruck, like two conspirators.

"You pour the coffee. I loathe it! I'm going! Good

27

night!" said the old woman, in a succession of sharp shots. And she scrambled out of the room.

There was a dead silence. At last he said:

"I'm afraid mother isn't well. I must persuade her to see a doctor."

"Yes!" said Cecilia.

The evening passed in silence. Robert and Ciss stayed on in the drawing-room, having lit a fire. Outside was cold rain. Each pretended to read. They did not want to separate. The evening passed with ominous mysteriousness, yet quickly.

At about ten o'clock, the door suddenly opened, and Pauline appeared, in a blue wrap. She shut the door behind her, and came to the fire. Then she looked at the two young people in hate, real hate.

"You two had better get married quickly," she said in an ugly voice. "It would look more decent; such a passionate pair of lovers!"

Robert looked up at her quietly.

"I thought you believed that cousins should not marry, mother," he said.

"I do! But you're not cousins. Your father was an Italian priest." Pauline held her daintily slippered foot to the fire, in an old coquettish gesture. Her body tried to repeat all the old graceful gestures. But the nerve had snapped, so it was a rather dreadful caricature.

"Is that really true, mother?" he asked.

"True! What do you think? He was a distinguished

28

man, or he wouldn't have been my lover. He was far too distinguished a man to have had you for a son. But that joy fell to me."

"How unfortunate all round," he said slowly.

"Unfortunate for you? *You* were lucky. It was *my* misfortune," she said acidly to him.

She was really a dreadful sight, like a piece of lovely Venetian glass that has been dropped, and gathered up again in horrible, sharp-edged fragments.

Suddenly she left the room again.

For a week it went on. She did not recover. It was as if every nerve in her body had suddenly started screaming in an insanity of discordance. The doctor came, and gave her sedatives, for she never slept. Without drugs, she never slept at all, only paced back and forth in her room, looking hideous and evil, reeking with malevolence. She could not bear to see either her son or her niece. Only when either of them came, she asked in pure malice:

"Well! When's the wedding? Have you celebrated the nuptials yet?"

At first Cecilia was stunned by what she had done. She realized vaguely that her aunt, once a definite thrust of condemnation had penetrated her beautiful armour, had just collapsed squirming inside her shell. It was too terrible. Ciss was almost terrified into repentance. Then she thought: This is what she always was. Now let her live the rest of her days in her true colours.

29

The Lovely Lady

But Pauline would not live long. She was literally shrivelling away. She kept her room, and saw no one. She had her mirrors taken away.

Robert and Cecilia sat a good deal together. The jeering of the mad Pauline had not driven them apart, as she had hoped. But Cecilia dared not confess to him what she had done.

"Do you think your mother ever loved anybody?" Ciss asked him tentatively, rather wistfully, one evening.

He looked at her fixedly.

"Herself!" he said at last.

"She didn't even *love* herself," said Ciss. "It was something else—what was it?" She lifted a troubled, utterly puzzled face to him.

"Power!" he said curtly.

"But what power?" she asked. "I don't understand."

"Power to feed on other lives," he said bitterly. "She was beautiful, and she fed on life. She has fed on me as she fed on Henry. She put a sucker into one's soul, and sucked up one's essential life."

"And don't you forgive her?"

"No."

"Poor Aunt Pauline!"

But even Ciss did not mean it. She was only aghast.

"I *know* I've got a heart," he said, passionately striking his breast. "But it's almost sucked dry. I *know* people who want power over others."

Ciss was silent; what was there to say?

30

The Lovely Lady

And two days later, Pauline was found dead in her bed, having taken too much veronal, for her heart was weakened. From the grave even she hit back at her son and her niece. She left Robert the noble sum of one thousand pounds; and Ciss one hundred. All the rest, with the nucleus of her valuable antiques, went to form the "Pauline Attenborough Museum."

Rawdon's Roof

Rawdon was the sort of man who said, privately, to his men friends, over a glass of wine after dinner: "No woman shall sleep again under my roof!"

He said it with pride, rather vaunting, pursing his lips. "Even my housekeeper goes home to sleep."

But the housekeeper was a gentle old thing of about sixty, so it seemed a little fantastic. Moreover the man had a wife, of whom he was secretly rather proud, as a piece of fine property, and with whom he kept up a very witty correspondence, epistolary, and whom he treated with humorous gallantry when they occasionally met for half-an-hour. Also he had a love affair going on. At least, if it wasn't a love affair, what was it? However!

"No, I've come to the determination that no woman shall ever sleep under my roof again—not even a female cat!"

One looked at the roof, and wondered what it had done amiss. Besides, it wasn't his roof. He only rented the house. What does a man mean, anyhow, when he says "my roof"? *My* roof! The only roof I am conscious of having, myself, is the top of my head. However, he hardly can have meant that no woman should sleep under the elegant dome of his skull. Though there's no telling. You see the top of a sleek head through a window, and you say: "By Jove, what a pretty girl's head!" And after all, when the individual comes out, it's in trousers.

The point, however, is that Rawdon said so emphatically—no, not emphatically, succinctly: "No woman shall ever again sleep under my roof." It was a case of futurity. No doubt he had had his ceilings whitewashed, and their memories put out. Or rather, repainted, for it was a handsome wooden ceiling. Anyhow, if ceilings have eyes, as walls have ears, then Rawdon had given his ceilings a new outlook, with a new coat of paint, and all memory of any woman's having slept under them—for, after all, in decent circumstances we sleep under ceilings, not under roofs— was wiped out for ever.

"And will you neither sleep under any woman's roof?"

That pulled him up rather short. He was not prepared to sauce his gander as he had sauced his goose. Even I could see the thought flitting through his mind, that some of his pleasantest holidays depended on the charm of his hostess. Even some of the nicest hotels were run by women.

"Ah! Well! That's not quite the same thing, you know. When one leaves one's own house one gives up the keys of circumstance, so to speak. But, as far as possible, I make it a rule not to sleep under a roof that

36

is openly, and obviously, and obtrusively a woman's roof!"

"Quite!" said I with a shudder. "So do I!"

Now I understood his mysterious love affair less than ever. He was never known to speak of this love affair: he did not even write about it to his wife. The lady—for she was a lady—lived only five minutes' walk from Rawdon. She had a husband, but he was in diplomatic service or something like that, which kept him occupied in the sufficiently far distance. Yes, far enough. And, as a husband, he was a complete diplomat. A balance of power. If he was entitled to occupy the wide field of the world, she, the other and contrasting power, might concentrate and consolidate her position at home.

She was a charming woman, too, and even a beautiful woman. She had two charming children, long-legged, stalky, clove-pink-half-opened sort of children. But really charming. And she was a woman with a certain mystery. She never talked. She never said anything about herself. Perhaps she suffered; perhaps she was frightfully happy, and made *that* her cause for silence. Perhaps she was wise enough even to be beautifully silent about her happiness. Certainly she never mentioned her sufferings, or even her trials; and certainly she must have a fair handful of the latter, for Alec Drummond sometimes fled home in the teeth of a gale of debts. He simply got through his own money and through hers, and, third and fatal stride, through other people's as well. Then something

had to be done about it. And Janet, dear soul, had to
put her hat on and take journeys. But she never said
anything of it. At least, she did just hint that Alec
didn't *quite* make enough money to meet expenses.
But after all, we don't go about with our eyes shut,
and Alec Drummond, whatever else he did, didn't
hide his prowess under a bushel.

Rawdon and he were quite friendly, but really!
None of them ever talked. Drummond didn't talk, he
just went off and behaved in his own way. And
though Rawdon would chat away till the small hours,
he never "talked." Not to his nearest male friend did
he ever mention Janet save as a very pleasant woman
and his neighbour: he admitted he adored her children. They often came to see him.

And one felt about Rawdon, he was making a mystery of something. And that was rather irritating. He
went every day to see Janet, and, of course, we saw
him going: going or coming. How can one help but
see? But he always went in the morning, at about
eleven, and did not stay for lunch; or he went in the
afternoon, and came home to dinner. Apparently he
was never there in the evening. Poor Janet, she lived
like a widow.

Very well, if Rawdon wanted to make it so blat-
antly obvious that it was only platonic, purely platonic, why wasn't he natural? Why didn't he say
simply: "I'm very fond of Janet Drummond, she is
my very dear friend"? Why did he sort of curl up
at the very mention of her name, and curdle into

silence; or else say rather forcedly: "Yes, she is a charming woman. I see a good deal of her, but chiefly for the children's sake. I'm devoted to the children!" Then he would look at one in such a curious way, as if he were hiding something. And after all, what was there to hide? If he was the woman's friend, why not? It could be a charming friendship. And if he were her lover, why, heaven bless me, he ought to have been proud of it, and showed just a glint, just an honest man's glint.

But no! never a glint of pride or pleasure in the relation either way. Instead of that, this rather theatrical reserve. Janet, it is true, was just as reserved. If she could, she avoided mentioning his name. Yet one knew, sure as houses, she felt something. One suspected her of being more in love with Rawdon than ever she had been with Alec. And one felt that there was a hush put upon it all. She had had a hush put upon her. By whom? By both the men? Or by Rawdon only? Or by Drummond? Was it for her husband's sake? Impossible! For her children's? But why? Her children were devoted to Rawdon.

It now had become the custom for them to go to him three times a week, for music. I don't mean he taught them the piano. Rawdon was a very refined musical amateur. He had them sing, in their delicate girlish voices, delicate little songs, and really he succeeded wonderfully with them; he made them so true, which children rarely are, musically, and so pure and effortless, like little flamelets of sound. It really was

39

rather beautiful and sweet of him. And he taught them *music*, the delicacy of the feel of it. They had a regular teacher for the practice.

Even the little girls, in their young little ways, were in love with Rawdon! So if their mother were in love too, in her ripened womanhood, why not?

Poor Janet! She was so still, and so elusive: the hush upon her! She was rather like a half-opened rose that somebody had tied a string round, so that it couldn't open any more. But why? Why? In her there was a real touch of mystery. One could never *ask* her, because one knew her heart was too keenly involved; or her pride.

Whereas there was, really, no mystery about Rawdon, refined and handsome and subtle as he was. He *had* no mystery; at least, to a man. What *he* wrapped himself up in was a certain amount of mystification.

Who wouldn't be irritated to hear a fellow saying, when for months and months he has been paying a daily visit to a lonely and very attractive woman— nay, lately even a twice-daily visit, even if always before sundown—to hear him say, pursing his lips after a sip of his own very moderate port: "I've taken a vow that no woman shall sleep under my roof again!"

I almost snapped out: "Oh, what the hell! And what about your Janet?" But I remembered in time, it was not *my* affair, and if he wanted to have his mystifications, let him have them.

If he meant he wouldn't have his wife sleep under

his roof again, that one could understand. They were really very witty with one another, he and she, but fatally and damnably married.

Yet neither wanted a divorce. And neither put the slightest claim to any control over the other's behaviour. He said: "Women live on the moon, men on the earth." And she said: "I don't mind in the least if he loves Janet Drummond, poor thing. It would be a change for him, from loving himself. And a change for her, if somebody loved her. . . ."

Poor Janet! But he wouldn't have her sleep under his roof, no, not for any money. And apparently he never slept under hers—if she could be said to have one. So what the deuce?

Of course, if they were friends, just friends, all right! But then in that case, why start talking about not having a woman sleep under your roof? Pure mystification!

The cat never came out of the bag. But one evening I distinctly heard it mewing inside its sack, and I even believe I saw a claw through the canvas.

It was in November—everything much as usual— myself pricking my ears to hear if the rain had stopped, and I could go home, because I was just a little bored about "cornemuse" music. I had been having dinner with Rawdon, and listening to him ever since on his favourite topic: not, of course, women, and why they shouldn't sleep under his roof, but fourteenth-century melody and windbag accompaniment.

The Lovely Lady

It was not late—not yet ten o'clock—but I was restless, and wanted to go home. There was no longer any sound of rain. And Rawdon was perhaps going to make a pause in his monologue.

Suddenly there was a tap at the door, and Rawdon's man, Hawken, edged in. Rawdon, who had been a major in some fantastic capacity during the war, had brought Hawken back with him. This fresh-faced man of about thirty-five appeared in the doorway with an intensely blank and bewildered look on his face. He was really an extraordinarily good actor.

"A lady, sir!" he said, with a look of utter blankness.

"A what?" snapped Rawdon.

"A lady!"—then with a most discreet drop in his voice: "Mrs. Drummond, sir!" He looked modestly down at his feet.

Rawdon went deathly white, and his lips quivered.

"Mrs. Drummond! Where?"

Hawken lifted his eyes to his master in a fleeting glance.

"I showed her into the dining-room, there being no fire in the drawing-room."

Rawdon got to his feet, and took two or three agitated strides. He could not make up his mind. At last he said, his lips working with agitation:

"Bring her in here."

Then he turned with a theatrical gesture to me.

"What this is all about, I *don't* know," he said.

"Let me clear out," said I, making for the door.

He caught me by the arm.

"No, for God's sake! For God's sake, stop and see me through!"

He gripped my arm till it really hurt, and his eyes were quite wild. I did not know my Olympic Rawdon.

Hastily I backed away to the side of the fire—we were in Rawdon's room, where the books and piano were—and Mrs. Drummond appeared in the doorway. She was much paler than usual, being a rather warm-coloured woman, and she glanced at me with big re-proachful eyes, as much as to say: You intruder! You interloper! For my part, I could do nothing but stare. She wore a black wrap, which I knew quite well, over her black dinner-dress.

"Rawdon!" she said, turning to him, and blotting out my existence from her consciousness. Hawken softly closed the door, and I could *feel* him standing on the threshold outside, listening keen as a hawk.

"Sit down, Janet," said Rawdon, with a grimace of a sour smile, which he could not get rid of once he had started it, so that his face looked very odd indeed, like a mask which he was unable either to fit on or take off. He had several conflicting expressions all at once, and they had all stuck.

She let her wrap slip back on her shoulders, and knitted her white fingers against her skirt, pressing down her arms, and gazing at him with a terrible gaze. I began to creep to the door.

Rawdon started after me.

43

"No, don't go! Don't go! I specially want you not to go," he said in extreme agitation.

I looked at her. She was looking at him with a heavy, sombre kind of stare. Me she absolutely ignored. Not for a second could she forgive me for existing on the earth. I slunk back to my post behind the leather arm-chair, as if hiding.

"Do sit down, Janet," he said to her again. "And have a smoke. What will you drink?"

"No, thanks!" she said, as if it were one word slurred out. "Nothanks."

And she proceeded again to fix him with that heavy, portentous stare.

He offered her a cigarette, his hand trembling as he held out the silver box.

"Nothanks!" she slurred out again, not even looking at the box, but keeping him fixed with that dark and heavy stare.

He turned away, making a great delay lighting a cigarette, with his back to her, to get out of the stream of that stare. He carefully went for an ash-tray, and put it carefully within reach—all the time trying not to be swept away on that stare. And she stood with her fingers locked, her straight, plump, handsome arms pressed downwards against her skirt, and she gazed at him.

He leaned his elbow on the mantelpiece abstractedly for a moment—then he started suddenly, and rang the bell. She turned her eyes from him for a moment, to watch his middle finger pressing the bell-button.

Then there was a tension of waiting, an interruption in the previous tension. We waited. Nobody came. Rawdon rang again.

"That's very curious!" he murmured to himself.— Hawken was usually so prompt. Hawken, not being a woman, slept under the roof, so there was no excuse for his not answering the bell. The tension in the room had now changed quality, owing to this new suspense. Poor Janet's sombre stare became gradually loosened, so to speak. Attention was divided. Where was Hawken? Rawdon rang the bell a third time, a long peal. And now Janet was no longer the centre of suspense. Where was Hawken? The question loomed large over every other.

"I'll just look in the kitchen," said I, making for the door.

"No, no. I'll go," said Rawdon.

But I was in the passage—and Rawdon was on my heels.

The kitchen was very tidy and cheerful, but empty; only a bottle of beer and two glasses stood on the table. To Rawdon the kitchen was as strange a world as to me—he never entered the servants' quarters. But to me it was curious that the bottle of beer was empty, and both the glasses had been used. I knew Rawdon wouldn't notice.

"That's very curious!" said Rawdon, meaning the absence of his man.

At that moment we heard a step on the servants' stairs, and Rawdon opened the door, to reveal

45

Hawken descending with an armful of sheets and things.

"What are you doing?"

"Why!—" and a pause. "I was airing the clean laundry, like—not to waste the fire last thing."

Hawken descended into the kitchen with a very flushed face and very bright eyes and rather ruffled hair, and proceeded to spread the linen on chairs before the fire.

"I hope I've not done wrong, sir," he said in his most winning manner. "Was you ringing?"

"Three times! Leave that linen, and bring a bottle of the fizz."

"I'm sorry, sir. You can't hear the bell from the front, sir."

It was perfectly true. The house was small, but it had been built for a very nervous author, and the servants' quarters were shut off, padded off from the rest of the house.

Rawdon said no more about the sheets and things, but he looked more peaked than ever.

We went back to the music-room. Janet had gone to the hearth, and stood with her hand on the mantel. She looked round at us, baffled.

"We're having a bottle of fizz," said Rawdon. "Do let me take your wrap."

"And where was Hawken?" she asked satirically.

"Oh, busy somewhere upstairs."

"He's a busy young man, that!" she said sardoni-

46

cally. And she sat uncomfortably on the edge of the chair where I had been sitting.

When Hawken came with the tray, she said:

"I'm not going to drink."

Rawdon appealed to me, so I took a glass. She looked inquiringly at the flushed and bright-eyed Hawken, as if she understood something.

The manservant left the room. We drank our wine, and the awkwardness returned.

"Rawdon!" she said suddenly, as if she were firing a revolver at him. "Alec came home tonight in a bigger mess than ever, and wanted to make love to me to get it off his mind. I can't stand it any more. I'm in love with you, and I simply can't stand Alec getting too near to me. He's dangerous when he's cross—and when he's worked up. So I just came here. I didn't see what else I could do."

She left off as suddenly as a machine-gun leaves off firing. We were just dazed.

"You are quite right," Rawdon began, in a vague and neutral tone. . . .

"I am, am I not?" she said eagerly.

"I'll tell you what I'll do," he said. "I'll go round to the hotel tonight, and you can stay here."

"Under the kindly protection of Hawken, you mean!" she said, with quiet sarcasm.

"Why!—I could send Mrs. Betts, I suppose," he said.

Mrs. Betts was his housekeeper.

"You couldn't stay and protect me yourself?" she said quietly.

"I! I! Why, I've made a vow—haven't I, Joe?"—he turned to me—"not to have any woman sleep under my roof again."—He got the mixed sour smile on his face.

She looked up at the ceiling for a moment, then lapsed into silence. Then she said:

"Sort of monastery, so to speak!"

And she rose and reached for her wrap, adding:

"I'd better go, then."

"Joe will see you home," he said.

She faced round on me.

"Do you mind *not* seeing me home, Mr. Bradley?" she said, gazing at me.

"Not if you don't want me," said I.

"Hawken will drive you," said Rawdon.

"Oh, no, he won't!" she said. "I'll walk. Good night."

"I'll get my hat," stammered Rawdon, in an agony. "Wait! Wait! The gate will be locked."

"It was open when I came," she said.

He rang for Hawken to unlock the iron doors at the end of the short drive, whilst he himself huddled into a greatcoat and scarf, fumbling for a flashlight.

"You won't go till I come back, will you?" he pleaded to me. "I'd be awfully glad if you'd stay the night. The sheets *will* be aired."

I had to promise—and he set off with an umbrella, in the rain, at the same time asking Hawken to take a flashlight and go in front. So that was how they went, in single file along the path over the fields to Mrs. Drummond's house, Hawken in front, with flashlight and umbrella, curving round to light up in front of Mrs. Drummond, who, with umbrella only, walked isolated between two lights, Rawdon shining his flashlight on her from the rear from under his umbrella. I turned indoors.

So that was over! At least, for the moment!

I thought I would go upstairs and see how damp the bed in the guest-chamber was, before I actually stayed the night with Rawdon. He never had guests—preferred to go away himself.

The guest-chamber was a good room across a passage and round a corner from Rawdon's room—its door just opposite the padded service-door. This latter service-door stood open, and a light shone through. I went into the spare bedroom, switching on the light.

To my surprise, the bed looked as if it had just been left—the sheets tumbled, the pillows pressed. I put in my hands under the bedclothes, and it was warm. Very curious!

As I stood looking round in mild wonder, I heard a voice call softly: "Joe!"

"Yes!" said I instinctively, and, though startled, strode at once out of the room and through the servants' door, towards the voice. Light shone from the open doorway of one of the servants' rooms.

There was a muffled little shriek, and I was standing looking into what was probably Hawken's bedroom,

49

and seeing a soft and pretty white leg and a very pretty feminine posterior very thinly dimmed in a rather short nightdress, just in the act of climbing into a narrow little bed, and, then arrested, the owner of the pretty posterior burying her face in the bedclothes, to be invisible, like the ostrich in the sand.

I discreetly withdrew, went downstairs and poured myself a glass of wine. And very shortly Rawdon returned, looking like Hamlet in the last Act.

He said nothing, neither did I. We sat and merely smoked. Only as he was seeing me upstairs to bed, in the now immaculate bedroom, he said pathetically:

"Why aren't women content to be what a man wants them to be?"

"Why aren't they!" said I wearily.

"I thought I had made everything clear," he said.

"You start at the wrong end," said I.

And as I said it, the picture came into my mind of the pretty feminine butt-end in Hawken's bedroom. Yes, Hawken made better starts, wherever he ended.

When he brought me my cup of tea in the morning, he was very soft and cat-like. I asked him what sort of day it was, and he asked me if I'd had a good night, and was I comfortable.

"Very comfortable!" said I. "But I turned you out, I'm afraid."

"Me, sir?" He turned on me a face of utter bewilderment.

But I looked him in the eye.

"Is your name Joe?" I asked him.

Rawdon's Roof

"You're right, sir."

"So is mine," said I. "However, I didn't see her face, so it's all right.—I suppose you *were* a bit tight, in that little bed!"

"Well, sir!" and he flashed me a smile of amazing impudence, and lowered his tone to utter confidence. "This is the best bed in the house, this is." And he touched it softly.

"You've not tried them all, surely?"

A look of indignant horror on his face!

"No, sir, indeed I haven't."

That day, Rawdon left for London, on his way to Tunis, and Hawken was to follow him. The roof of his house looked just the same.

The Drummonds moved too—went away somewhere, and left a lot of unsatisfied tradespeople behind.

The Rocking-Horse Winner

There was a woman who was beautiful, who started with all the advantages, yet she had no luck. She married for love, and the love turned to dust. She had bonny children, yet she felt they had been thrust upon her, and she could not love them. They looked at her coldly, as if they were finding fault with her. And hurriedly she felt she must cover up some fault in herself. Yet what it was that she must cover up she never knew. Nevertheless, when her children were present, she always felt the centre of her heart go hard. This troubled her, and in her manner she was all the more gentle and anxious for her children, as if she loved them very much. Only she herself knew that at the centre of her heart was a hard little place that could not feel love, no, not for anybody. Everybody else said of her: "She is such a good mother. She adores her children." Only she herself, and her children themselves, knew it was not so. They read it in each other's eyes.

There were a boy and two little girls. They lived in a pleasant house, with a garden, and they had discreet servants, and felt themselves superior to anyone in the neighbourhood.

The Lovely Lady

Although they lived in style, they felt always an anxiety in the house. There was never enough money. The mother had a small income, and the father had a small income, but not nearly enough for the social position which they had to keep up. The father went in to town to some office. But though he had good prospects, these prospects never materialized. There was always the grinding sense of the shortage of money, though the style was always kept up.

At last the mother said: "I will see if *I* can't make something." But she did not know where to begin. She racked her brains, and tried this thing and the other, but could not find anything successful. The failure made deep lines come into her face. Her children were growing up, they would have to go to school. There must be more money, there must be more money. The father, who was always very handsome and expensive in his tastes, seemed as if he never *would* be able to do anything worth doing. And the mother, who had a great belief in herself, did not succeed any better, and her tastes were just as expensive.

And so the house came to be haunted by the unspoken phrase: *There must be more money! There must be more money!* The children could hear it all the time, though nobody said it aloud. They heard it at Christmas, when the expensive and splendid toys filled the nursery. Behind the shining modern rocking-horse, behind the smart doll's-house, a voice would start whispering: "There *must* be more money! There *must* be more money!" And the children would stop playing, to listen for a moment. They would look into each other's eyes, to see if they had all heard. And each one saw in the eyes of the other two that they too had heard. "There *must* be more money! There *must* be more money!"

It came whispering from the springs of the still-swaying rocking-horse, and even the horse, bending his wooden, champing head, heard it. The big doll, sitting so pink and smirking in her new pram, could hear it quite plainly, and seemed to be smirking all the more self-consciously because of it. The foolish puppy, too, that took the place of the teddy-bear, he was looking so extraordinarily foolish for no other reason but that he heard the secret whisper all over the house: "There *must* be more money!"

Yet nobody ever said it aloud. The whisper was everywhere, and therefore no one spoke it. Just as no one ever says: "We are breathing!" in spite of the fact that breath is coming and going all the time.

"Mother," said the boy Paul one day, "why don't we keep a car of our own? Why do we always use uncle's, or else a taxi?"

"Because we're the poor members of the family," said the mother.

"But why *are* we, mother?"

"Well—I suppose," she said slowly and bitterly, "it's because your father has no luck."

The boy was silent for some time.

"Is luck money, mother?" he asked, rather timidly.

"No, Paul. Not quite. It's what causes you to have money."

"Oh!" said Paul vaguely. "I thought when Uncle Oscar said *filthy lucker*, it meant money."

"*Filthy lucre* does mean money," said the mother. "But it's lucre, not luck."

"Oh!" said the boy. "Then what *is* luck, mother?"

"It's what causes you to have money. If you're lucky you have money. That's why it's better to be born lucky than rich. If you're rich, you may lose your money. But if you're lucky, you will always get more money."

"Oh! Will you? And is father not lucky?"

"Very unlucky, I should say," she said bitterly.

The boy watched her with unsure eyes.

"Why?" he asked.

"I don't know. Nobody ever knows why one person is lucky and another unlucky."

"Don't they? Nobody at all? Does *nobody* know?"

"Perhaps God. But He never tells."

"He ought to, then. And aren't you lucky either, mother?"

"I can't be, if I married an unlucky husband."

"But by yourself, aren't you?"

"I used to think I was, before I married. Now I think I am very unlucky indeed."

"Why?"

"Well—never mind! Perhaps I'm not really," she said.

The child looked at her, to see if she meant it. But

The Rocking-Horse Winner

he saw, by the lines of her mouth, that she was only trying to hide something from him.

"Well, anyhow," he said stoutly, "I'm a lucky person."

"Why?" said his mother, with a sudden laugh.

He stared at her. He didn't even know why he had said it.

"God told me," he asserted, brazening it out.

"I hope He did, dear!" she said, again with a laugh, but rather bitter.

"He did, mother!"

"Excellent!" said the mother, using one of her husband's exclamations.

The boy saw she did not believe him; or, rather, that she paid no attention to his assertion. This angered him somewhat, and made him want to compel her attention.

He went off by himself, vaguely, in a childish way, seeking for the clue to "luck." Absorbed, taking no heed of other people, he went about with a sort of stealth, seeking inwardly for luck. He wanted luck, he wanted it, he wanted it. When the two girls were playing dolls in the nursery, he would sit on his big rocking-horse, charging madly into space, with a frenzy that made the little girls peer at him uneasily. Wildly the horse careered, the waving dark hair of the boy tossed, his eyes had a strange glare in them. The little girls dared not speak to him.

When he had ridden to the end of his mad little journey, he climbed down and stood in front of his rocking-horse, staring fixedly into its lowered face. Its red mouth was slightly open, its big eye was wide and glassy-bright.

"Now!" he would silently command the snorting steed. "Now, take me to where there is luck! Now take me!"

And he would slash the horse on the neck with the little whip he had asked Uncle Oscar for. He *knew* the horse could take him to where there was luck, if only he forced it. So he would mount again, and start on his furious ride, hoping at last to get there. He knew he could get there.

"You'll break your horse, Paul!" said the nurse.

"He's always riding like that! I wish he'd leave off!" said his elder sister Joan.

But he only glared down on them in silence. Nurse gave him up. She could make nothing of him. Anyhow he was growing beyond her.

One day his mother and his Uncle Oscar came in when he was on one of his furious rides. He did not speak to them.

"Hallo, you young jockey! Riding a winner?" said his uncle.

"Aren't you growing too big for a rocking-horse? You're not a very little boy any longer, you know," said his mother.

But Paul only gave a blue glare from his big, rather close-set eyes. He would speak to nobody when he was in full tilt. His mother watched him with an anxious expression on her face.

The Rocking-Horse Winner

At last he suddenly stopped forcing his horse into the mechanical gallop, and slid down.

"Well, I got there!" he announced fiercely, his blue eyes still flaring, and his sturdy long legs straddling apart.

"Where did you get to?" asked his mother.

"Where I wanted to go," he flared back at her.

"That's right, son!" said Uncle Oscar. "Don't you stop till you get there. What's the horse's name?"

"He doesn't have a name," said the boy.

"Gets on without all right?" asked the uncle.

"Well, he has different names. He was called Sansovino last week."

"Sansovino, eh? Won the Ascot. How did you know his name?"

"He always talks about horse-races with Bassett," said Joan.

The uncle was delighted to find that his small nephew was posted with all the racing news. Bassett, the young gardener, who had been wounded in the left foot in the war and had got his present job through Oscar Cresswell, whose batman he had been, was a perfect blade of the "turf." He lived in the racing events, and the small boy lived with him.

Oscar Cresswell got it all from Bassett.

"Master Paul comes and asks me, so I can't do more than tell him, sir," said Bassett, his face terribly serious, as if he were speaking of religious matters.

"And does he ever put anything on a horse he fancies?"

The Lovely Lady

"Well—I don't want to give him away—he's a young sport, a fine sport, sir. Would you mind asking him himself? He sort of takes a pleasure in it, and perhaps he'd feel I was giving him away, sir, if you don't mind."

Bassett was serious as a church.

The uncle went back to his nephew, and took him off for a ride in the car.

"Say, Paul, old man, do you ever put anything on a horse?" the uncle asked.

The boy watched the handsome man closely.

"Why, do you think I oughtn't to?" he parried.

"Not a bit of it! I thought perhaps you might give me a tip for the Lincoln."

The car sped on into the country, going down to Uncle Oscar's place in Hampshire.

"Honour bright?" said the nephew.

"Honour bright, son!" said the uncle.

"Well, then, Daffodil."

"Daffodil! I doubt it, sonny. What about Mirza?"

"I only know the winner," said the boy. "That's Daffodil."

"Daffodil, eh?"

There was a pause. Daffodil was an obscure horse comparatively.

"Uncle!"

"Yes, son?"

"You won't let it go any further, will you? I promised Bassett."

The Rocking-Horse Winner

"Bassett be damned, old man! What's he got to do with it?"

"We're partners. We've been partners from the first. Uncle, he lent me my first five shillings, which I lost. I promised him, honour bright, it was only between me and him; only you gave me that ten-shilling note I started winning with, so I thought you were lucky. You won't let it go any further, will you?"

The boy gazed at his uncle from those big, hot, blue eyes, set rather close together. The uncle stirred and laughed uneasily.

"Right you are, son! I'll keep your tip private. Daffodil, eh? How much are you putting on him?"

"All except twenty pounds," said the boy. "I keep that in reserve."

The uncle thought it a good joke.

"You keep twenty pounds in reserve, do you, you young romancer? What are you betting, then?"

"I'm betting three hundred," said the boy gravely. "But it's between you and me, Uncle Oscar! Honour bright?"

The uncle burst into a roar of laughter.

"It's between you and me all right, you young Nat Gould," he said, laughing. "But where's your three hundred?"

"Bassett keeps it for me. We're partners."

"You are, are you! And what is Bassett putting on Daffodil?"

The Lovely Lady

"He won't go quite as high as I do, I expect. Perhaps he'll go a hundred and fifty."

"What, pennies?" laughed the uncle.

"Pounds," said the child, with a surprised look at his uncle. "Bassett keeps a bigger reserve than I do."

Between wonder and amusement Uncle Oscar was silent. He pursued the matter no further, but he determined to take his nephew with him to the Lincoln races.

"Now, son," he said, "I'm putting twenty on Mirza, and I'll put five for you on any horse you fancy. What's your pick?"

"Daffodil, uncle."

"No, not the fiver on Daffodil!"

"I should if it was my own fiver," said the child.

"Good! Good! Right you are! A fiver for me and a fiver for you on Daffodil."

The child had never been to a race-meeting before, and his eyes were blue fire. He pursed his mouth tight, and watched. A Frenchman just in front had put his money on Lancelot. Wild with excitement, he flayed his arms up and down, yelling *Lancelot! Lancelot!* in his French accent.

Daffodil came in first, Lancelot second, Mirza third. The child, flushed and with eyes blazing, was curiously serene. His uncle brought him four five-pound notes, four to one.

"What am I to do with these?" he cried, waving them before the boy's eyes.

"I suppose we'll talk to Bassett," said the boy. "I

expect I have fifteen hundred now; and twenty in reserve; and this twenty."

His uncle studied him for some moments.

"Look here, son!" he said. "You're not serious about Bassett and that fifteen hundred, are you?"

"Yes, I am. But it's between you and me, uncle. Honour bright!"

"Honour bright all right, son! But I must talk to Bassett."

"If you'd like to be a partner, uncle, with Bassett and me, we could all be partners. Only, you'd have to promise, honour bright, uncle, not to let it go beyond us three. Bassett and I are lucky, and you must be lucky, because it was your ten shillings I started winning with. . . ."

Uncle Oscar took both Bassett and Paul into Richmond Park for an afternoon, and there they talked.

"It's like this, you see, sir," Bassett said. "Master Paul would get me talking about racing events, spinning yarns, you know, sir. And he was always keen on knowing if I'd made or if I'd lost. It's about a year since, now, that I put five shillings on Blush of Dawn for him—and we lost. Then the luck turned, with that ten shillings he had from you, that we put on Singhalese. And since that time, it's been pretty steady, all things considering. What do you say, Master Paul?"

"We're all right when we're sure," said Paul. "It's when we're not quite sure that we go down."

"Oh, but we're careful then," said Bassett.

"But when are you *sure*?" smiled Uncle Oscar.

"It's Master Paul, sir," said Bassett, in a secret, religious voice. "It's as if he had it from heaven. Like Daffodil, now, for the Lincoln. That was as sure as eggs."

"Did you put anything on Daffodil?" asked Oscar Cresswell.

"Yes, sir. I made my bit."

"And my nephew?"

Bassett was obstinately silent, looking at Paul.

"I made twelve hundred, didn't I, Bassett? I told uncle I was putting three hundred on Daffodil."

"That's right," said Bassett, nodding.

"But where's the money?" asked the uncle.

"I keep it safe locked up, sir. Master Paul he can have it any minute he likes to ask for it."

"What, fifteen hundred pounds?"

"And twenty! And *forty*, that is, with the twenty he made on the course."

"It's amazing!" said the uncle.

"If Master Paul offers you to be partners, sir, I would, if I were you; if you'll excuse me," said Bassett.

Oscar Cresswell thought about it.

"I'll see the money," he said.

They drove home again, and sure enough, Bassett came round to the garden-house with fifteen hundred pounds in notes. The twenty pounds reserve was left with Joe Glee, in the Turf Commission deposit.

The Rocking-Horse Winner

"You see, it's all right, uncle, when I'm *sure*! Then we go strong, for all we're worth. Don't we, Bassett?"

"We do that, Master Paul."

"And when are you sure?" said the uncle, laughing.

"Oh, well, sometimes I'm *absolutely* sure, like about Daffodil," said the boy; "and sometimes I have an idea; and sometimes I haven't even an idea, have I, Bassett? Then we're careful, because we mostly go down."

"You do, do you! And when you're sure, like about Daffodil, what makes you sure, sonny?"

"Oh, well, I don't know," said the boy uneasily. "I'm sure, you know, uncle; that's all."

"It's as if he had it from heaven, sir," Bassett reiterated.

"I should say so!" said the uncle.

But he became a partner. And when the Leger was coming on, Paul was "sure" about Lively Spark, which was a quite inconsiderable horse. The boy insisted on putting a thousand on the horse, Bassett went for five hundred, and Oscar Cresswell two hundred. Lively Spark came in first, and the betting had been ten to one against him. Paul had made ten thousand.

"You see," he said, "I was absolutely sure of him."

Even Oscar Cresswell had cleared two thousand.

"Look here, son," he said, "this sort of thing makes me nervous."

"It needn't, uncle! Perhaps I shan't be sure again for a long time."

"But what are you going to do with your money?" asked the uncle.

"Of course," said the boy, "I started it for mother. She said she had no luck, because father is unlucky, so I thought if *I* was lucky, it might stop whispering."

"What might stop whispering?"

"Our house. I *hate* our house for whispering."

"What does it whisper?"

"Why—why"—the boy fidgeted—"why, I don't know. But it's always short of money, you know, uncle."

"I know it, son, I know it."

"You know people send mother writs, don't you, uncle?"

"I'm afraid I do," said the uncle.

"And then the house whispers, like people laughing at you behind your back. It's awful, that is! I thought if I was lucky . . ."

"You might stop it," added the uncle.

The boy watched him with big blue eyes, that had an uncanny cold fire in them, and he said never a word.

"Well, then!" said the uncle. "What are we doing?"

"I shouldn't like mother to know I was lucky," said the boy.

"Why not, son?"

"She'd stop me."

"I don't think she would."

"Oh!"—and the boy writhed in an odd way—"I *don't* want her to know, uncle."

The Rocking-Horse Winner

"All right, son! We'll manage it without her knowing."

They managed it very easily. Paul, at the other's suggestion, handed over five thousand pounds to his uncle, who deposited it with the family lawyer, who was then to inform Paul's mother that a relative had put five thousand pounds into his hands, which sum was to be paid out a thousand pounds at a time, on the mother's birthday, for the next five years.

"So she'll have a birthday present of a thousand pounds for five successive years," said Uncle Oscar. "I hope it won't make it all the harder for her later."

Paul's mother had her birthday in November. The house had been "whispering" worse than ever lately, and, even in spite of his luck, Paul could not bear up against it. He was very anxious to see the effect of the birthday letter, telling his mother about the thousand pounds.

When there were no visitors, Paul now took his meals with his parents, as he was beyond the nursery control. His mother went into town nearly every day. She had discovered that she had an odd knack of sketching furs and dress materials, so she worked secretly in the studio of a friend who was the chief "artist" for the leading drapers. She drew the figures of ladies in furs and ladies in silk and sequins for the newspaper advertisements. This young woman artist earned several thousand pounds a year, but Paul's mother only made several hundreds, and she was again dissatisfied. She so wanted to be first in something, and she did not succeed, even in making sketches for drapery advertisements.

She was down to breakfast on the morning of her birthday. Paul watched her face as she read her letters. He knew the lawyer's letter. As his mother read it, her face hardened and became more expressionless. Then a cold, determined look came on her mouth. She hid the letter under the pile of others, and said not a word about it.

"Didn't you have anything nice in the post for your birthday, mother?" said Paul.

"Quite moderately nice," she said, her voice cold and absent.

She went away to town without saying more.

But in the afternoon Uncle Oscar appeared. He said Paul's mother had had a long interview with the lawyer, asking if the whole five thousand could not be advanced at once, as she was in debt.

"What do you think, uncle?" said the boy.

"I leave it to you, son."

"Oh, let her have it, then! We can get some more with the other," said the boy.

"A bird in the hand is worth two in the bush, laddie!" said Uncle Oscar.

"But I'm sure to *know* for the Grand National; or the Lincolnshire; or else the Derby. I'm sure to know for *one* of them," said Paul.

So Uncle Oscar signed the agreement, and Paul's mother touched the whole five thousand. Then some-

The Rocking-Horse Winner

thing very curious happened. The voices in the house suddenly went mad, like a chorus of frogs on a spring evening. There were certain new furnishings, and Paul had a tutor. He was *really* going to Eton, his father's school, in the following autumn. There were flowers in the winter, and a blossoming of the luxury Paul's mother had been used to. And yet the voices in the house, behind the sprays of mimosa and almond blossom, and from under the piles of iridescent cushions, simply trilled and screamed in a sort of ecstasy: "There *must* be more money! Oh-h-h; there *must* be more money. Oh, now, now-w! Now-w-w—there *must* be more money!—more than ever! More than ever!"

It frightened Paul terribly. He studied away at his Latin and Greek with his tutors. But his intense hours were spent with Bassett. The Grand National had gone by: he had not "known," and had lost a hundred pounds. Summer was at hand. He was in agony for the Lincoln. But even for the Lincoln he didn't "know," and he lost fifty pounds. He became wild-eyed and strange, as if something were going to explode in him.

"Let it alone, son! Don't you bother about it!" urged Uncle Oscar. But it was as if the boy couldn't really hear what his uncle was saying.

"I've got to know for the Derby! I've got to know for the Derby!" the child reiterated, his big blue eyes blazing with a sort of madness.

The Lovely Lady

His mother noticed how overwrought he was.

"You'd better go to the seaside. Wouldn't you like to go now to the seaside, instead of waiting? I think you'd better," she said, looking down at him anxiously, her heart curiously heavy because of him.

But the child lifted his uncanny blue eyes.

"I couldn't possibly go before the Derby, mother!" he said. "I couldn't possibly!"

"Why not?" she said, her voice becoming heavy when she was opposed. "Why not? You can still go from the seaside to see the Derby with your Uncle Oscar, if that's what you wish. No need for you to wait here. Besides, I think you care too much about these races. It's a bad sign. My family has been a gambling family, and you won't know till you grow up how much damage it has done. But it has done damage. I shall have to send Bassett away, and ask Uncle Oscar not to talk racing to you, unless you promise to be reasonable about it; go away to the seaside and forget it. You're all nerves!"

"I'll do what you like, mother, so long as you don't send me away till after the Derby," the boy said.

"Send you away from where? Just from this house?"

"Yes," he said, gazing at her.

"Why, you curious child, what makes you care about this house so much, suddenly? I never knew you loved it."

He gazed at her without speaking. He had a secret

72

within a secret, something he had not divulged, even to Bassett or to his Uncle Oscar.

But his mother, after standing undecided and a little bit sullen for some moments, said:

"Very well, then! Don't go to the seaside till after the Derby, if you don't wish it. But promise me you won't let your nerves go to pieces. Promise you won't think so much about horse-racing and *events*, as you call them!"

"Oh, no," said the boy casually. "I won't think much about them, mother. You needn't worry. I wouldn't worry, mother, if I were you."

"If you were me and I were you," said his mother, "I wonder what we *should* do!"

"But you know you needn't worry, mother, don't you?" the boy repeated.

"I should be awfully glad to know it," she said wearily.

"Oh, well, you *can*, you know. I mean, you *ought* to know you needn't worry," he insisted.

"Ought I? Then I'll see about it," she said.

Paul's secret of secrets was his wooden horse, that which had no name. Since he was emancipated from a nurse and a nursery-governess, he had had his rocking-horse removed to his own bedroom at the top of the house.

"Surely, you're too big for a rocking-horse!" his mother had remonstrated.

"Well, you see, mother, till I can have a *real* horse,

73

The Lovely Lady

I like to have *some* sort of animal about," had been his quaint answer.

"Do you feel he keeps you company?" she laughed.

"Oh, yes! He's very good, he always keeps me company, when I'm there," said Paul.

So the horse, rather shabby, stood in an arrested prance in the boy's bedroom.

The Derby was drawing near, and the boy grew more and more tense. He hardly heard what was spoken to him, he was very frail, and his eyes were really uncanny. His mother had sudden strange seizures of uneasiness about him. Sometimes, for half-an-hour, she would feel a sudden anxiety about him that was almost anguish. She wanted to rush to him at once, and know he was safe.

Two nights before the Derby, she was at a big party in town, when one of her rushes of anxiety about her boy, her first-born, gripped her heart till she could hardly speak. She fought with the feeling, might and main, for she believed in commonsense. But it was too strong. She had to leave the dance and go downstairs to telephone to the country. The children's nursery-governess was terribly surprised and startled at being rung up in the night.

"Are the children all right, Miss Wilmot?"

"Oh, yes, they are quite all right."

"Master Paul? Is he all right?"

"He went to bed as right as a trivet. Shall I run up and look at him?"

"No," said Paul's mother reluctantly. "No! Don't

74

The Rocking-Horse Winner

trouble. It's all right. Don't sit up. We shall be home fairly soon." She did not want her son's privacy intruded upon.

"Very good," said the governess.

It was about one o'clock when Paul's mother and father drove up to their house. All was still. Paul's mother went to her room and slipped off her white fur cloak. She had told her maid not to wait up for her. She heard her husband downstairs, mixing a whisky-and-soda.

And then, because of the strange anxiety at her heart, she stole upstairs to her son's room. Noiselessly she went along the upper corridor. Was there a faint noise? What was it?

She stood, with arrested muscles, outside his door, listening. There was a strange, heavy, and yet not loud noise. Her heart stood still. It was a soundless noise, yet rushing and powerful. Something huge, in violent, hushed motion. What was it? What in God's name was it? She ought to know. She felt that she knew the noise. She knew what it was.

Yet she could not place it. She couldn't say what it was. And on and on it went, like a madness.

Softly, frozen with anxiety and fear, she turned the door-handle.

The room was dark. Yet in the space near the window, she heard and saw something plunging to and fro. She gazed in fear and amazement.

Then suddenly she switched on the light, and saw her son, in his green pyjamas, madly surging on the

75

rocking-horse. The blaze of light suddenly lit him up, as he urged the wooden horse, and lit her up, as she stood, blonde, in her dress of pale green and crystal, in the doorway.

"Paul!" she cried. "Whatever are you doing?"

"It's Malabar!" he screamed, in a powerful, strange voice. "It's Malabar!"

His eyes blazed at her for one strange and senseless second, as he ceased urging his wooden horse. Then he fell with a crash to the ground, and she, all her tormented motherhood flooding upon her, rushed to gather him up.

But he was unconscious, and unconscious he remained, with some brain-fever. He talked and tossed, and his mother sat stonily by his side.

"Malabar! It's Malabar! Bassett, Bassett, I *know*! It's Malabar!"

So the child cried, trying to get up and urge the rocking-horse that gave him his inspiration.

"What does he mean by Malabar?" asked the heart-frozen mother.

"I don't know," said the father stonily.

"What does he mean by Malabar?" she asked her brother Oscar.

"It's one of the horses running for the Derby," was the answer.

And, in spite of himself, Oscar Cresswell spoke to Bassett, and himself put a thousand on Malabar: at fourteen to one.

The third day of the illness was critical: they were

waiting for a change. The boy, with his rather long, curly hair, was tossing ceaselessly on the pillow. He neither slept nor regained consciousness, and his eyes were like blue stones. His mother sat, feeling her heart had gone, turned actually into a stone.

In the evening, Oscar Cresswell did not come, but Bassett sent a message, saying could he come up for one moment, just one moment? Paul's mother was very angry at the intrusion, but on second thought she agreed. The boy was the same. Perhaps Bassett might bring him to consciousness.

The gardener, a shortish fellow with a little brown moustache, and sharp little brown eyes, tiptoed into the room, touched his imaginary cap to Paul's mother, and stole to the bedside, staring with glittering, smallish eyes, at the tossing, dying child.

"Master Paul!" he whispered. "Master Paul! Malabar came in first all right, a clean win. I did as you told me. You've made over seventy thousand pounds, you have; you've got over eighty thousand. Malabar came in all right, Master Paul."

"Malabar! Malabar! Did I say Malabar, mother? Did I say Malabar? Do you think I'm lucky, mother? I knew Malabar, didn't I? Over eighty thousand pounds! I call that lucky, don't you, mother? Over eighty thousand pounds! I knew, didn't I know I knew? Malabar came in all right. If I ride my horse till I'm sure, then I tell you, Bassett, you can go as high as you like. Did you go for all you were worth, Bassett?"

The Lovely Lady

"I went a thousand on it, Master Paul."

"I never told you, mother, that if I can ride my horse, and *get there*, then I'm absolutely sure—oh, absolutely! Mother, did I ever tell you? I *am* lucky!"

"No, you never did," said the mother.

But the boy died in the night.

And even as he lay dead, his mother heard her brother's voice saying to her: "My God, Hester, you're eighty-odd thousand to the good, and a poor devil of a son to the bad. But, poor devil, poor devil, he's best gone out of a life where he rides his rocking-horse to find a winner."

Mother and Daughter

Mother and Daughter

irginia Bodoin had a good job: she was head
of a department in a certain government office, held a
responsible position, and earned, to imitate Balzac and
be precise about it, seven hundred and fifty pounds a
year. That is already something. Rachel Bodoin, her
mother, had an income of about six hundred a year,
on which she had lived in the capitals of Europe since
the effacement of a never very important husband.

Now, after some years of virtual separation and
"freedom," mother and daughter once more thought
of settling down. They had become, in course of
time, more like a married couple than mother and
daughter. They knew one another very well indeed,
and each was a little "nervous" of the other. They
had lived together and parted several times. Virginia
was now thirty, and she didn't look like marrying.
For four years she had been as good as married to
Henry Lubbock, a rather spoilt young man who was
musical. Then Henry let her down: for two reasons.
He couldn't stand her mother. Her mother couldn't
stand him. And anybody whom Mrs. Bodoin could
not stand she managed to sit on, disastrously. So Henry
had writhed horribly, feeling his mother-in-law sit-

ting on him tight, and Virginia, after all, in a helpless sort of family loyalty, sitting alongside her mother. Virginia didn't really want to sit on Henry. But when her mother egged her on, she couldn't help it. For ultimately, her mother had power over her: a strange *female* power, nothing to do with parental authority. Virginia had long thrown parental authority to the winds. But her mother had another, much subtler form of domination, female and thrilling, so that when Rachel said: Let's squash him! Virginia had to rush wickedly and gleefully to the sport. And Henry knew quite well when he was being squashed. So that was one of his reasons for going back on Vinny.—He called her Vinny, to the superlative disgust of Mrs. Bodoin, who always corrected him: My daughter *Virginia*——

The second reason was, again to be Balzacian, that Virginia hadn't a sou of her own. Henry had a sorry two hundred and fifty. Virginia, at the age of twenty-four, was already earning four hundred and fifty. But she was earning them. Whereas Henry managed to earn about twelve pounds per annum, by his precious music. He had realized that he would find it hard to earn more. So that marrying, except with a wife who could keep him, was rather out of the question. Vinny would inherit her mother's money. But then Mrs. Bodoin had the health and muscular equipment of the Sphinx. She would live for ever, seeking whom she might devour, and devouring him. Henry lived with Vinny for two years, in the married sense of the

82

words; and Vinny felt they *were* married, minus a mere ceremony. But Vinny had her mother always in the background; often as far back as Paris or Biarritz, but still, within letter reach. And she never realized the funny little grin that came on her own elvish face when her mother, even in a letter, spread her skirts and calmly sat on Henry. She never realized that in spirit she promptly and mischievously sat on him too; she could no more have helped it than the tide can help turning to the moon. And she did not dream that he felt it, and was utterly mortified in his masculine vanity. Women, very often, hypnotize one another, and then, hypnotized, they proceed gently to wring the neck of the man they think they are loving with all their hearts. Then they call it utter perversity on his part, that he doesn't like having his neck wrung. They think he is repudiating a heart-felt love. For they are hypnotized. Women hypnotize one another, without knowing it.

In the end, Henry backed out. He saw himself being simply reduced to nothingness by two women, an old witch with muscles like the Sphinx, and a young, spellbound witch, lavish, elvish, and weak, who utterly spoilt him but who ate his marrow.

Rachel would write from Paris: My dear Virginia, as I had a windfall in the way of an investment, I am sharing it with you. You will find enclosed my cheque for twenty pounds. No doubt you will be needing it to buy Henry a suit of clothes, since the spring is apparently come, and the sunlight may be tempted to show him up for what he is worth. I don't want my daughter going around with what is presumably a street-corner musician, but please pay the tailor's bill yourself, or you may have to do it over again later.— Henry got a suit of clothes, but it was as good as a shirt of Nessus, eating him away with subtle poison.

So he backed out. He didn't jump out, or bolt, or carve his way out at the sword's point. He sort of faded out, distributing his departure over a year or more. He was fond of Vinny, and he could hardly do without her, and he was sorry for her. But at length he couldn't see her apart from her mother. She was a young, weak, spendthrift witch, accomplice of her tough-clawed witch of a mother.

Henry made other alliances, got a good hold on elsewhere, and gradually extricated himself. He saved his life, but he had lost, he felt, a good deal of his youth and marrow. He tended now to go fat, a little puffy, somewhat insignificant. And he had been handsome and striking-looking.

The two witches howled when he was lost to them. Poor Virginia was really half crazy; she didn't know what to do with herself. She had a violent recoil from her mother. Mrs. Bodoin was filled with furious contempt for her daughter: that she should let such a hooked fish slip out of her hands! that she should allow such a person to turn her down!—"I don't quite see my daughter seduced and thrown over by a sponging individual such as Henry Lubbock," she wrote.

Mother and Daughter

"But if it has happened, I suppose it is somebody's fault. . . ."

There was a mutual recoil, which lasted nearly five years. But the spell was not broken. Mrs. Bodoin's mind never left her daughter, and Virginia was ceaselessly aware of her mother, somewhere in the universe. They wrote, and met at intervals, but they kept apart in recoil.

The spell, however, was between them, and gradually it worked. They felt more friendly. Mrs. Bodoin came to London. She stayed in the same quiet hotel with her daughter: Virginia had had two rooms in an hotel for the past three years. And, at last, they thought of taking an apartment together.

Virginia was now over thirty. She was still thin and odd and elvish, with a very slight and piquant cast in one of her brown eyes, and she still had her odd, twisted smile, and her slow, rather deep-toned voice, that caressed a man like the stroking of subtle fingertips. Her hair was still a natural tangle of curls, a bit dishevelled. She still dressed with a natural elegance which tended to go wrong and a tiny bit sluttish. She still might have a hole in her expensive and perfectly new stockings, and still she might have to take off her shoes in the drawing-room, if she came to tea, and sit there in her stockinged feet. True, she had elegant feet: she was altogether elegantly shaped. But it wasn't that. It was neither coquetry nor vanity. It was simply that, after having gone to a good shoemaker and paid five guineas for a pair of perfectly simple and natural shoes, made to her feet, the said shoes would hurt her excruciatingly, when she had walked half a mile in them, and she would simply have to take them off, even if she sat on the kerb to do it. It was a fatality. There was a touch of the *gamin* in her very feet, a certain sluttishness that wouldn't let them stay properly in nice proper shoes. She practically always wore her mother's old shoes.—Of course, I go through life in mother's old shoes. If she died and left me without a supply, I suppose I should have to go in a bathchair, she would say, with her odd twisted little grin. She was so elegant, and yet a slut. It was her charm, really.

Just the opposite of her mother. They could wear each other's shoes and each other's clothes, which seemed remarkable, for Mrs. Bodoin seemed so much the bigger of the two. But Virginia's shoulders were broad, if she was thin; she had a strong frame, even when she looked a frail rag.

Mrs. Bodoin was one of those women of sixty or so, with a terrible inward energy and a violent sort of vitality. But she managed to hide it. She sat with perfect repose, and folded hands. One thought: What a calm woman! Just as one may look at the snowy summit of a quiescent volcano, in the evening light, and think: What peace!

It was a strange *muscular* energy which possessed Mrs. Bodoin, as it possesses, curiously enough, many women over fifty, and is usually distasteful in its

86

manifestations. Perhaps it accounts for the lassitude of the young.

But Mrs. Bodoin recognized the bad taste in her energetic coevals, so she cultivated repose. Her very way of pronouncing the word, in two syllables: re-pòse, making the second syllable run on into the twilight, showed how much suppressed energy she had. Faced with the problem of iron-grey hair and black eyebrows, she was too clever to try dyeing herself back into youth. She studied her face, her whole figure, and decided that it was *positive*. There was no denying it. There was no wispiness, no hollowness, no limp frail blossom-on-a-bending-stalk about her. Her figure, though not stout, was full, strong, and *cambré*. Her face had an aristocratic arched nose, aristocratic, who-the-devil-are-you grey eyes, and cheeks rather long but also rather full. Nothing appealing or youthfully skittish here.

Like an independent woman, she used her wits, and decided most emphatically not to be either youthful or skittish or appealing. She would keep her dignity, for she was fond of it. She was positive. She liked to be positive. She was used to her positivity. So she would just *be* positive.

She turned to the positive period: to the eighteenth century, to Voltaire, to Ninon de l'Enclos and the Pompadour, to Madame la Duchesse and Monsieur le Marquis. She decided that she was not much in the line of la Pompadour or la Duchesse, but almost exactly in the line of Monsieur le Marquis. And she

87

was right. With hair silvering to white, brushed back clean from her positive brow and temples, cut short, but sticking out a little behind, with her rather full, pink face and thin black eyebrows plucked to two fine, superficial crescents, her arching nose and her rather full insolent eyes she was perfectly eighteenth century, the early half. That she was Monsieur le Marquis rather than Madame la Marquise made her really modern.

Her appearance was perfect. She wore delicate combinations of grey and pink, maybe with a darkening iron-grey touch, and her jewels were of soft old coloured paste. Her bearing was a sort of alert repose, very calm, but very assured. There was, to use a vulgarism, no getting past her.

She had a couple of thousand pounds she could lay hands on. Virginia, of course, was always in debt. But, after all, Virginia was not to be sniffed at. She made seven hundred and fifty a year.

Virginia was oddly clever, and not clever. She didn't *really* know anything, because anything and everything was interesting to her for the moment, and she picked it up at once. She picked up languages with extraordinary ease; she was fluent in a fortnight. This helped her enormously with her job. She could prattle away with heads of industry, let them come from where they liked. But she didn't *know* any language, not even her own. She picked things up in her sleep, so to speak, without knowing anything about them.

Mother and Daughter

And this made her popular with men. With all her curious facility, they didn't feel small in front of her, because she was like an instrument. She had to be prompted. Some man had to set her in motion, and then she worked, really cleverly. She could collect the most valuable information. She was very useful. She worked with men, spent most of her time with men, her friends were practically all men. She didn't feel easy with women.

Yet she had no lover, nobody seemed eager to marry her, nobody seemed eager to come close to her at all. Mrs. Bodoin said: I'm afraid Virginia is a one-man woman. I am a one-man woman. So was my mother, and so was my grandmother. Virginia's father was the only man in my life, the only one. And I'm afraid Virginia is the same, tenacious. Unfortunately, the man was what he was, and her life is just left there.

Henry had said, in the past, that Mrs. Bodoin wasn't a one-man woman, she was a no-man woman, and that if she could have had her way, everything male would have been wiped off the face of the earth, and only the female element left.

However, Mrs. Bodoin thought that it was now time to make a move. So she and Virginia took a quite handsome apartment in one of the old Bloomsbury Squares, fitted it up and furnished it with extreme care, and with some quite lovely things, got in a very good man, an Austrian, to cook, and they set up married life together, mother and daughter.

The Lovely Lady

At first it was rather thrilling. The two reception-rooms, looking down on the dirty old trees of the Square garden, were of splendid proportions, and each with three great windows coming down low, almost to the level of the knees. The chimney-piece was late eighteenth century. Mrs. Bodoin furnished the rooms with a gentle suggestion of Louis Seize merged with Empire, without keeping to any particular style. But she had, saved from her own home, a really remarkable Aubusson carpet. It looked almost new, as if it had been woven two years ago, and was startling, yet somehow rather splendid, as it spread its rose-red borders and wonderful florid array of silver-grey and gold-grey roses, lilies, and gorgeous swans and trumpeting volutes away over the floor. Very æsthetic people found it rather loud; they preferred the worn, dim yellowish Aubusson in the big bedroom. But Mrs. Bodoin loved her drawing-room carpet. It was positive, but it was not vulgar. It had a certain grand air in its floridity. She felt it gave her a proper footing. And it behaved very well with her painted cabinets and grey-and-gold brocade chairs and big Chinese vases, which she liked to fill with big flowers: single Chinese peonies, big roses, great tulips, orange lilies. The dim room of London, with all its atmospheric colour, would stand the big, free, fisticuffing flowers.

Virginia, for the first time in her life, had the pleasure of making a home. She was again entirely under her mother's spell, and swept away, thrilled to her marrow. She had had no idea that her mother had got such treasures as the carpets and painted cabinets and brocade chairs up her sleeve: many of them the débris of the Fitzpatrick home in Ireland, Mrs. Bodoin being a Fitzpatrick. Almost like a child, like a bride, Virginia threw herself into the business of fixing up the rooms. "Of course, Virginia, I consider this is *your* apartment," said Mrs. Bodoin. "I am nothing but your *dame de compagnie*, and shall carry out your wishes entirely, if you will only express them."

Of course, Virginia expressed a few, but not many. She introduced some wild pictures bought from impecunious artists whom she patronized. Mrs. Bodoin thought the pictures positive about the wrong things, but as far as possible, she let them stay, looking on them as the necessary element of modern ugliness. But by that element of modern ugliness, wilfully so, it was easy to see the things that Virginia had introduced into the apartment.

Perhaps nothing goes to the head like setting up house. You can get drunk on it. You feel you are creating something. Nowadays it is no longer the "home," the domestic nest. It is "my rooms," or "my house," the great garment which reveals and clothes "my personality." Mrs. Bodoin, deliberately scheming for Virginia, kept moderately cool over it, but even she was thrilled to the marrow, and of an intensity and ferocity with the decorators and furnishers, astonishing. But Virginia was just all the time tipsy with it, as if she had touched some magic button on the grey wall of life, and with an Open Sesame! her lovely and coloured rooms had begun to assemble out of fairyland. It was far more vivid and wonderful to her than if she had inherited a duchy.

The mother and daughter, the mother in a sort of faded russet crimson and the daughter in silver, began to entertain. They had, of course, mostly men. It filled Mrs. Bodoin with a sort of savage impatience to entertain women. Besides, most of Virginia's acquaintances were men. So there were dinners and well-arranged evenings.

It went well, but something was missing. Mrs. Bodoin wanted to be gracious, so she held herself rather back. She stayed a little distant, was calm, reposed, eighteenth century, and determined to be a foil to the clever and slightly elvish Virginia. It was a pose, and, alas, it stopped something. She was very nice with the men, no matter what her contempt of them. But the men were uneasy with her: afraid.

What they all felt, all the men guests, was that *for them*, nothing really happened. Everything that happened was between mother and daughter. All the flow was between mother and daughter. A subtle, hypnotic spell encompassed the two women, and, try as they might, the men were shut out. More than one young man, a little dazzled, *began* to fall in love with Virginia. But it was impossible. Not only was he shut out, he was, in some way, annihilated. The spontaneity was killed in his bosom. While the two women sat, brilliant and rather wonderful, in magnetic connexion

Mother and Daughter

at opposite ends of the table, like two witches, a double Circe turning the men not into swine—the men would have liked that well enough—but into lumps.

It was tragic. Because Mrs. Bodoin wanted Virginia to fall in love and marry. She really wanted it, and she attributed Virginia's lack of forthcoming to the delinquent Henry. She never realized the hypnotic spell, which of course encompassed her as well as Virginia, and made men just an impossibility to both women, mother and daughter alike.

At this time, Mrs. Bodoin hid her humour. She had a really marvellous faculty of humorous imitation. She could imitate the Irish servants from her old home, or the American women who called on her, or the modern ladylike young men, the asphodels, as she called them: "Of course you know the asphodel is a kind of onion! Oh, yes, just an overbred onion": who wanted, with their murmuring voices and peeping under their brows, to make her feel very small and very bourgeois. She could imitate them all with a humour that was really touched with genius. But it was devastating. It demolished the objects of her humour so absolutely, smashed them to bits with a ruthless hammer, pounded them to nothing so terribly, that it frightened people, particularly men. It frightened men off.

So she hid it. She hid it. But there it was, up her sleeve, her merciless, hammer-like humour, which just smashed its object on the head and left him brained. She tried to disown it. She tried to pretend, even to

93

The Lovely Lady

Virginia, that she had the gift no more. But in vain; the hammer hidden up her sleeve hovered over the head of every guest, and every guest felt his scalp creep, and Virginia felt her inside creep with a little, mischievous, slightly idiotic grin, as still another fool male was mystically knocked on the head. It was a sort of uncanny sport.

No, the plan was not going to work, the plan of having Virginia fall in love and marry. Of course the men *were* such lumps, such *œufs farcis*. There was one, at least, that Mrs. Bodoin had real hopes of. He was a healthy and normal and very good-looking boy of good family, with no money, alas, but clerking to the House of Lords and very hopeful, and not very clever, but simply in love with Virginia's cleverness. He was just the one Mrs. Bodoin would have married for herself. True, he was only twenty-six, to Virginia's thirty-one. But he had rowed in the Oxford eight, and adored horses, talked horses adorably, and was simply infatuated by Virginia's cleverness. To him Virginia had the finest mind on earth. She was as wonderful as Plato, but infinitely more attractive, because she was a woman, and winsome with it. Imagine a winsome Plato with untidy curls and the tiniest little brown-eyed squint and just a hint of woman's pathetic need for a protector, and you may imagine Adrian's feeling for Virginia. He adored her on his knees, but he felt he could protect her.

"Of course, he's just a very nice *boy*!" said Mrs. Bodoin. "He's a boy, and that's all you can say. And

94

he always will be a boy. But that's the very nicest kind of man, the only kind you can live with: the eternal boy. Virginia, aren't you attracted to him?"

"Yes, mother! I think he's an awfully nice *boy*, as you say," replied Virginia, in her rather slow, musical, whimsical voice. But the mocking little curl in the intonation put the lid on Adrian. Virginia was not marrying a nice *boy*! She could be malicious, too, against her mother's taste. And Mrs. Bodoin let escape her a faint gesture of impatience.

For she had been planning her own retreat, planning to give Virginia the apartment outright, and half of her own income, if she would marry Adrian. Yes, the mother was already scheming how best she could live with dignity on three hundred a year, once Virginia was happily married to that most attractive if slightly brainless *boy*.

A year later, when Virginia was thirty-two, Adrian, who had married a wealthy American girl and been transferred to a job in the legation at Washington in the meantime, faithfully came to see Virginia as soon as he was in London, faithfully kneeled at her feet, faithfully thought her the most wonderful spiritual being, and faithfully felt that she, Virginia, could have done wonders with him, which wonders would now never be done, for he had married in the meantime.

Virginia was looking haggard and worn. The scheme of a *ménage à deux* with her mother had not succeeded. And now, work was telling on the younger woman. It is true, she was amazingly facile. But facility wouldn't get her all the way. She had to earn her money, and earn it hard. She had to slog, and she had to concentrate. While she could work by quick intuition and without much responsibility, work thrilled her. But as soon as she had to get down to it, as they say, grip and slog and concentrate, in a really responsible position, it wore her out terribly. She had to do it all off her nerves. She hadn't the same sort of fighting power as a man. Where a man can summon his old Adam in him to fight through his work, a woman has to draw on her nerves, and on her nerves alone. For the old Eve in her will have nothing to do with such work. So that mental responsibility, mental concentration, mental slogging wear out a woman terribly, especially if she is head of a department, and not working *for* somebody.

So poor Virginia was worn out. She was thin as a rail. Her nerves were frayed to bits. And she could never forget her beastly work. She would come home at tea-time speechless and done for. Her mother, tortured by the sight of her, longed to say: Has anything gone wrong, Virginia? Have you had anything particularly trying at the office today?—But she learned to hold her tongue and say nothing. The question would be the last straw to Virginia's poor overwrought nerves, and there would be a little scene which, despite Mrs. Bodoin's calm and forbearance, offended the elder woman to the quick. She had learned, by bitter experience, to leave her child alone, as one would leave a frail tube of vitriol alone. But, of course she could not

Mother and Daughter

keep her *mind* off Virginia. That was impossible. And poor Virginia, under the strain of work and the strain of her mother's awful ceaseless mind, was at the very end of her strength and resources.

Mrs. Bodoin had always disliked the fact of Virginia's doing a job. But now she hated it. She hated the whole government office with violent and virulent hate. Not only was it undignified for Virginia to be tied up there, but it was turning her, Mrs. Bodoin's daughter, into a thin, nagging, fearsome old maid. Could anything be more utterly English and humiliating to a well-born Irishwoman?

After a long day attending to the apartment, skilfully darning one of the brocade chairs, polishing the Venetian mirrors to her satisfaction, selecting flowers, doing certain shopping and housekeeping, attending perfectly to everything, then receiving callers in the afternoon, with never-ending energy, Mrs. Bodoin would go up from the drawing-room after tea and write a few letters, take her bath, dress with great care—she enjoyed attending to her person—and come down to dinner as fresh as a daisy, but far more energetic than that quiet flower. She was ready now for a full evening.

She was conscious, with gnawing anxiety, of Virginia's presence in the house, but she did not see her daughter till dinner was announced. Virginia slipped in, and away to her room unseen, never going into the drawing-room to tea. If Mrs. Bodoin heard her daughter's key in the latch, she quickly retired into one of

97

the rooms till Virginia was safely through. It was too much for poor Virginia's nerves even to catch sight of anybody in the house, when she came in from the office. Bad enough to hear the murmur of visitors' voices behind the drawing-room door.

And Mrs. Bodoin would wonder: How is she? How is she tonight? I wonder what sort of a day she's had?—And this thought would roam prowling through the house, to where Virginia was lying on her back in her room. But the mother would have to consume her anxiety till dinner-time. And then Virginia would appear, with black lines under her eyes, thin, tense, a young woman out of an office, the stigma upon her: badly dressed, a little acid in humour, with an impaired digestion, not interested in anything, blighted by her work. And Mrs. Bodoin, humiliated at the very sight of her, would control herself perfectly, say nothing but the mere smooth nothings of casual speech, and sit in perfect form presiding at a carefully cooked dinner thought out entirely to please Virginia. Then Virginia hardly noticed what she ate.

Mrs. Bodoin was pining for an evening with life in it. But Virginia would lie on the couch and put on the loud-speaker. Or she would put a humorous record on the gramophone, and be amused, and hear it again, and be amused, and hear it again, six times, and six times be amused by a mildly funny record that Mrs. Bodoin now knew off by heart. "Why, Virginia, I could repeat that record over to you, if you wished it, without your troubling to wind up that gramophone."—And Virginia, after a pause in which she seemed not to have heard what her mother said, would reply: "I'm sure you could, mother." And that simple speech would convey such volumes of contempt for all that Rachel Bodoin was or ever could be or ever had been, contempt for her energy, her vitality, her mind, her body, her very existence, that the elder woman would curl. It seemed as if the ghost of Robert Bodoin spoke out of the mouth of the daughter, in deadly venom.—Then Virginia would put on the record for the seventh time.

During the second ghastly year, Mrs. Bodoin realized that the game was up. She was a beaten woman, a woman without object or meaning any more. The hammer of her awful female humour, which had knocked so many people on the head, all the people, in fact, that she had come into contact with, had at last flown backwards and hit herself on the head. For her daughter was her other self, her *alter ego*. The secret and the meaning and the power of Mrs. Bodoin's whole life lay in the hammer, that hammer of her living humour which knocked everything on the head. That had been her lust and her passion, knocking everybody and everything humorously on the head. She had felt inspired in it: it was a sort of mission. And she had hoped to hand on the hammer to Virginia, her clever, unsolid but still actual daughter, Virginia. Virginia was the continuation of Rachel's own self. Virginia was Rachel's *alter ego*, her other self.

But, alas, it was a half-truth. Virginia had had a father. This fact, which had been utterly ignored by

99

the mother, was gradually brought home to her by the curious recoil of the hammer. Virginia was her father's daughter. Could anything be more unseemly, horrid, more perverse in the natural scheme of things? For Robert Bodoin had been fully and deservedly knocked on the head by Rachel's hammer. Could anything, then, be more disgusting than that he should resurrect again in the person of Mrs. Bodoin's own daughter, her own *alter ego* Virginia, and start hitting back with a little spiteful hammer that was David's pebble against Goliath's battle-axe!

But the little pebble was mortal. Mrs. Bodoin felt it sink into her brow, her temple, and she was finished. The hammer fell nerveless from her hand.

The two women were now mostly alone. Virginia was too tired to have company in the evening. So there was the gramophone or loud-speaker, or else silence. Both women had come to loathe the apartment. Virginia felt it was the last grand act of bullying on her mother's part: she felt bullied by the assertive Aubusson carpet, by the beastly Venetian mirrors, by the big overcultured flowers. She even felt bullied by the excellent food, and longed again for a Soho restaurant and her two poky shabby rooms in the hotel. She loathed the apartment; she loathed everything. But she had not the energy to move. She had not the energy to do anything. She crawled to her work, and, for the rest, she lay flat, gone.

It was Virginia's worn-out inertia that really finished Mrs. Bodoin. That was the pebble that broke the bone

Mother and Daughter

of her temple: "To have to attend my daughter's funeral, and accept the sympathy of all her fellow-clerks in her office, no, that is a final humiliation which I must spare myself. No! If Virginia must be a lady clerk, she must be it henceforth on her own responsibility. I will retire from her existence."

Mrs. Bodoin had tried hard to persuade Virginia to give up her work and come and live with her. She had offered her half her income. In vain. Virginia stuck to her office.

Very well! So be it!—The apartment was a fiasco; Mrs. Bodoin was longing, longing to tear it to pieces again. One last and final blow of the hammer!—"Virginia, don't you think we'd better get rid of this apartment, and live around as we used to? Don't you think we'll do that?"—"But all the money you've put into it? And the lease for ten years!" cried Virginia, in a kind of inertia.—"Never mind! We had the pleasure of making it. And we've had as much pleasure out of living in it as we shall ever have. Now we'd better get rid of it—quickly—don't you think?"

Mrs. Bodoin's arms were twitching to snatch the pictures off the walls, roll up the Aubusson carpet, take the china out of the ivory-inlaid cabinet there and then, at that very moment.

"Let us wait till Sunday before we decide," said Virginia.

"Till Sunday! Four days! As long as that? Haven't we already decided in our own minds?" said Mrs. Bodoin.

The Lovely Lady

"We'll wait till Sunday, anyhow," said Virginia.

The next evening, the Armenian came to dinner. Virginia called him Arnold, with the French pronunciation, Arnault. Mrs. Bodoin, who barely tolerated him, and could never get his name, which seemed to have a lot of bouyoums in it, called him either the Armenian, or the Rahat Lakoum, after the name of the sweetmeat, or simply The Turkish Delight.

"Arnault is coming to dinner tonight, mother."

"Really! The Turkish Delight is coming here to dinner? Shall I provide anything special?"—Her voice sounded as if she would suggest snails in aspic.

"I don't think so."

Virginia had seen a good deal of the Armenian at the office, when she had to negotiate with him on behalf of the Board of Trade. He was a man of about sixty, a merchant, had been a millionaire, was ruined during the war, but was now coming on again, and represented trade in Bulgaria. He wanted to negotiate with the British Government, and the British Government sensibly negotiated with him: at first through the medium of Virginia. Now things were going satisfactorily between Monsieur Arnault, as Virginia called him, and the Board of Trade, so that a sort of friendship had followed the official relations.

The Turkish Delight was sixty, grey-haired, and fat. He had numerous grandchildren growing up in Bulgaria, but he was a widower. He had a grey moustache cut like a brush, and glazed brown eyes over which hung heavy lids with white lashes. His manner was humble, but in his bearing there was a certain dogged conceit. One notices the combination sometimes in Jews. He had been very wealthy and kow-towed to; he had been ruined and humiliated, terribly humiliated; and now, doggedly, he was rising up again, his sons backing him, away in Bulgaria. One felt he was not alone. He had his sons, his family, his tribe behind him, away in the Near East.

He spoke bad English, but fairly fluent guttural French. He did not speak much, but he sat. He sat, with his short, fat thighs, as if for eternity, *there*. There was a strange potency in his fat immobile sitting, as if his posterior were connected with the very centre of the earth. And his brain, spinning away at the one point in question, business, was very agile. Business absorbed him. But not in a nervous, personal way. Somehow the family, the tribe was always felt behind him. It was business for the family, the tribe.

With the English he was humble, for the English like such aliens to be humble, and he had had a long schooling from the Turks. And he was always an outsider. Nobody would ever take any notice of him in society. He would just be an outsider, *sitting*.

"I hope, Virginia, you won't ask that Turkish-carpet gentleman when we have other people. *I* can bear it," said Mrs. Bodoin. "Some people might mind."

"Isn't it hard when you can't choose your own company in your own house," mocked Virginia.

"No! *I* don't care. I can meet anything; and I'm sure, in the way of selling Turkish carpets, your acquaintance is very good. But I don't suppose you look on him as a personal friend . . . ?"

"I do. I like him quite a lot."

"Well . . . ! as you will. But consider your *other* friends."

Mrs. Bodoin was really mortified this time. She looked on the Armenian as one looks on the fat Levantine in a fez who tries to sell one hideous tapestries at Port Said, or on the sea-front at Nice, as being outside the class of human beings, and in the class of insects. That he had been a millionaire, and might be a millionaire again, only added venom to her feeling of disgust at being forced into contact with such scum. She could not even squash him, or annihilate him. In scum, there is nothing to squash, for scum is only the unpleasant residue of that which was never anything but squashed.

However, she was not quite just. True, he was fat, and he sat, with short thighs, like a toad, as if seated for a toad's eternity. His colour was of a dirty sort of paste, his brown eyes were glazed under heavy lids. And he never spoke until spoken to, waiting in his toad's silence, like a slave.

But his thick, fine white hair, which stood up on his head like a soft brush, was curiously virile. And his curious small hands, of the same soft dull paste, had a peculiar, fat, soft masculine breeding of their own. And his dull brown eye could glint with the subtlety of serpents, under the white brush of eyelash. He was tired, but he was not defeated. He had fought, and

Mother and Daughter

won, and lost, and was fighting again, always at a disadvantage. He belonged to a defeated race which accepts defeat, but which gets its own back by cunning. He was the father of sons, the head of a family, one of the heads of a defeated but indestructible tribe. He was not alone, and so you could not lay your finger on him. His whole consciousness was patriarchal and tribal. And somehow, he was humble, but he was indestructible.

At dinner he sat half-effaced, humble, yet with the conceit of the humble. His manners were perfectly good, rather French. Virginia chattered to him in French, and he replied with that peculiar nonchalance of the boulevards, which was the only manner he could command when speaking French. Mrs. Bodoin understood, but she was what one would call a heavy-footed linguist, so when she said anything, it was intensely in English. And the Turkish Delight replied in his clumsy English, hastily. It was not his fault that French was being spoken. It was Virginia's.

He was very humble, conciliatory, with Mrs. Bodoin. But he cast at her sometimes that rapid glint of a reptilian glance as if to say: Yes! I see you! You are a handsome figure. As an *objet de vertu* you are almost perfect.—Thus his connoisseur's, antique-dealer's eye would appraise her. But then his thick white eyebrows would seem to add: But what, under holy Heaven, are you as a woman? You are neither wife nor mother nor mistress, you have no perfume of sex, you are more dreadful than a Turkish soldier or an English official.

The Lovely Lady

No man on earth could embrace you. You are a ghoul, you are a strange genie from the underworld!—And he would secretly invoke the holy names, to shield him.

Yet he was in love with Virginia. He saw, first and foremost, the child in her, as if she were a lost child in the gutter, a waif with a faint, fascinating cast in her brown eyes, waiting till someone would pick her up. A fatherless waif! And he was tribal father, father through all the ages.

Then, on the other hand, he knew her peculiar disinterested cleverness in affairs. That, too, fascinated him: that odd, almost second-sight cleverness about business, and entirely impersonal, entirely in the air. It seemed to him very strange. But it would be an immense help to him in his schemes. He did not really understand the English. He was at sea with them. But with her, he would have a clue to everything. For she was, finally, quite a somebody among these English, these English officials.

He was about sixty. His family was established, in the East, his grandsons were growing up. It was necessary for him to live in London, for some years. This girl would be useful. She had no money, save what she would inherit from her mother. But he would risk that; she would be an investment in his business. And then the apartment. He liked the apartment extremely. He recognized the *cachet*, and the lilies and swans of the Aubusson carpet really did something to him. Virginia said to him: Mother gave me the apartment.— So he looked on that as safe. And finally, Virginia was almost a virgin, probably quite a virgin, and, as far as the paternal oriental male like himself was concerned, entirely virgin. He had a very small idea of the silly puppy-sexuality of the English, so different from the prolonged male voluptuousness of his own pleasures. And last of all, he was physically lonely, getting old, and tired.

Virginia, of course, did not know why she liked being with Arnault. Her cleverness was amazingly stupid when it came to life, to living. She said he was "quaint." She said his nonchalant French of the boulevards was "amusing." She found his business cunning "intriguing," and the glint in his dark glazed eyes, under the white, thick lashes, "sheiky." She saw him quite often, had tea with him in his hotel, and motored with him one day down to the sea.

When he took her hand in his own soft still hands, there was something so caressing, so possessive in his touch, so strange and positive in his leaning towards her, that, though she trembled with fear, she was helpless.—"But you are so thin, dear little thin thing, you need repose, repose, for the blossom to open, poor little blossom, to become a little fat!" he said in his French.

She quivered, and was helpless. It certainly was quaint! He was so strange and positive, he seemed to have all the power. The moment he realized that she would succumb into his power, he took full charge of the situation, he lost all his hesitation and his humility. He did not want just to make love to her: he wanted to marry her, for all his multifarious reasons. And he must make himself master of her.

He put her hand to his lips, and seemed to draw her life to his in kissing her thin hand. "The poor child is tired, she needs repose, she needs to be caressed and cared for," he said in his French. And he drew nearer to her.

She looked up in dread at his glinting, tired dark eyes under the white lashes. But he used all his will, looking back at her heavily and calculating that she must submit. And he brought his body quite near to her, and put his hand softly on her face, and made her lay her face against his breast, as he soothingly stroked her arm with his other hand. "Dear little thing! dear little thing! Arnault loves her so dearly! Arnault loves her! Perhaps she will marry her Arnault. Dear little girl, Arnault will put flowers in her life, and make her life perfumed with sweetness and content."

She leaned against his breast and let him caress her. She gave a fleeting, half poignant, half vindictive thought to her mother. Then she felt in the air the sense of destiny, destiny. Oh, so nice, not to have to struggle. To give way to destiny.

"Will she marry her old Arnault? Eh? Will she marry him?" he asked in a soothing, caressing voice, at the same time compulsive.

She lifted her head and looked at him: the thick white brows, the glinting, tired dark eyes. How queer and comic! How comic to be in his power! And he was looking a little baffled.

"Shall I?" she said, with her mischievous twist of a grin.

"Mais oui!" he said, with all the sang-froid of his old eyes. "Mais oui! Je te contenterai, tu le verras."

"Tu me contenteras!" she said, with a flickering smile of real amusement at his assurance. "Will you really content me?"

"But surely! I assure it you. And you will marry me?"

"You must tell mother," she said, and hid wickedly against his waistcoat again, while the male pride triumphed in him.

Mrs. Bodoin had no idea that Virginia was intimate with the Turkish Delight; she did not inquire into her daughter's movements. During the famous dinner, she was calm and a little aloof, but entirely self-possessed. When, after coffee, Virginia left her alone with the Turkish Delight, she made no effort at conversation, only glanced at the rather short, stout man in correct dinner-jacket, and thought how his sort of fatness called for a fez and the full muslin breeches of a bazaar merchant in *The Thief of Bagdad*.

"Do you really prefer to smoke a hookah?" she asked him, with a slow drawl.

"What is a hookah, please?"

"One of those water-pipes. Don't you all smoke them, in the East?"

He only looked mystified and humble, and silence resumed. She little knew what was simmering inside his stillness.

"Madame," he said, "I want to ask you something."

"You do? Then why not ask it?" came her slightly melancholy drawl.

"Yes! It is this. I wish I may have the honour to marry your daughter. She is willing."

There was a moment's blank pause. Then Mrs. Bodoin leant towards him from her distance, with curious portentousness.

"What was that you said?" she asked. "Repeat it!"

"I wish I may have the honour to marry your daughter. She is willing to take me."

His dark, glazed eyes looked at her, then glanced away again. Still leaning forward, she gazed fixedly on him, as if spellbound, turned to stone. She was wearing pink topaz ornaments, but he judged they were paste, moderately good.

"Did I hear you say she is willing to take you?" came the slow, melancholy, remote voice.

"Madame, I think so," he said, with a bow.

"I think we'll wait till she comes," she said, leaning back.

There was silence. She stared at the ceiling. He looked closely round the room, at the furniture, at the china in the ivory-inlaid cabinet.

"I can settle five thousand pounds on Mademoiselle Virginia, Madame," came his voice. "Am I correct to assume that she will bring this apartment and its appointments into the marriage settlement?"

Absolute silence. He might as well have been on

Mother and Daughter

the moon. But he was a good sitter. He just sat until Virginia came in.

Mrs. Bodoin was still staring at the ceiling. The iron had entered her soul finally and fully. Virginia glanced at her, but said: "Have a whisky-and-soda, Arnault?"

He rose and came towards the decanters, and stood beside her: a rather squat, stout man with white head, silent with misgiving. There was the fizz of the siphon; then they came to their chairs.

"Arnault has spoken to you, mother?" said Virginia.

Mrs. Bodoin sat up straight, and gazed at Virginia with big, owlish eyes, haggard. Virginia was terrified, yet a little thrilled. Her mother was beaten.

"Is it true, Virginia, that you are *willing* to marry this—oriental gentleman?" asked Mrs. Bodoin slowly.

"Yes, mother, quite true," said Virginia, in her teasing soft voice.

Mrs. Bodoin looked owlish and dazed.

"May I be excused from having any part in it, or from having anything to do with your future *husband* —I mean having any business to transact with him?" she asked dazedly, in her slow, distinct voice.

"Why, of course!" said Virginia, frightened, smiling oddly.

There was a pause. Then Mrs. Bodoin, feeling old and haggard, pulled herself together again.

"Am I to understand that your future husband would like to possess this apartment?" came her voice.

Virginia smiled quickly and crookedly. Arnault just

III

sat, planted on his posterior, and heard. She reposed on him.

"Well—perhaps!" said Virginia. "Perhaps he would like to know that I possessed it." She looked at him.

Arnault nodded gravely.

"And do you *wish* to possess it?" came Mrs. Bodoin's slow voice. "Is it your intention to *inhabit* it, with your *husband*?" She put eternities into her long, stressed words.

"Yes, I think it is," said Virginia. "You know you *said* the apartment was mine, mother."

"Very well! It shall be so. I shall send my lawyer to this—oriental gentleman, if you will leave written instructions on my writing-table. May I ask when you think of getting—*married*?"

"When do you think, Arnault?" said Virginia.

"Shall it be, in two weeks?" he said, sitting erect, with his fists on his knees.

"In about a fortnight, mother," said Virginia.

"I have heard! In two weeks! Very well! In two weeks everything shall be at your disposal. And now, please excuse me." She rose, made a slight general bow, and moved calmly and dimly from the room. It was killing her, that she could not shriek aloud and beat that Levantine out of the house. But she couldn't. She had imposed the restraint on herself.

Arnault stood and looked with glistening eyes round the room. It would be his. When his sons came to England, here he would receive them.

He looked at Virginia. She too was white and

haggard, now. And she flung away from him, as if in resentment. She resented the defeat of her mother. She was still capable of dismissing him for ever, and going back to her mother.

"Your mother is a wonderful lady," he said, going to Virginia and taking her hand. "But she has no husband to shelter her, she is unfortunate. I am sorry she will be alone. I should be happy if she would like to stay here with us."

The sly old fox knew what he was about.

"I'm afraid there's no hope of that," said Virginia, with a return to her old irony.

She sat on the couch, and he caressed her softly and paternally, and the very incongruity of it, there in her mother's drawing-room, amused her. And because he saw that the things in the drawing-room were handsome and valuable, and now they were his, his blood flushed and he caressed the thin girl at his side with passion, because she represented these valuable surroundings, and brought them to his possession. And he said: "And with me you will be very comfortable, very content, oh, I shall make you content, not like madame your mother. And you will get fatter, and bloom like the rose. I shall make you bloom like the rose. And shall we say next week, hein? Shall it be next week, next Wednesday, that we marry? Wednesday is a good day. Shall it be then?"

"Very well!" said Virginia, caressed again into a luxurious sense of destiny, reposing on fate, having to make no effort, no more effort, all her life.

Mrs. Bodoin moved into an hotel next day, and came into the apartment to pack up and extricate herself and her immediate personal belongings only when Virginia was necessarily absent. She and her daughter communicated by letter, as far as was necessary.

And in five days' time Mrs. Bodoin was clear. All business that could be settled was settled, all her trunks were removed. She had five trunks, and that was all. Denuded and outcast, she would depart to Paris, to live out the rest of her days.

The last day, she waited in the drawing-room till Virginia should come home. She sat there in her hat and street things, like a stranger.

"I just waited to say good-bye," she said. "I leave in the morning for Paris. This is my address. I think everything is settled; if not, let me know and I'll attend to it. Well, good-bye!—and I hope you'll be *very happy*!"

She dragged out the last words sinisterly; which restored Virginia, who was beginning to lose her head.

"Why, I think I may be," said Virginia, with the twist of a smile.

"I shouldn't wonder," said Mrs. Bodoin pointedly and grimly. "I think the Armenian grandpapa knows very well what he's about. You're just the harem type, after all." The words came slowly, dropping, each with a plop! of deep contempt.

"I suppose I am! Rather fun!" said Virginia. "But I wonder where I got it? Not from you, mother . . ." she drawled mischievously.

Mother and Daughter

"I should say *not*."

"Perhaps daughters go by contraries, like dreams," mused Virginia wickedly. "All the harem was left out of you, so perhaps it all had to be put back into me."

Mrs. Bodoin flashed a look at her.

"You have *all* my *pity*!" she said.

"Thank you, dear. You have just a bit of mine."

The Blue Moccasins

The fashion in women changes nowadays even faster than women's fashions. At twenty, Lina M'Leod was almost painfully modern. At sixty, almost obsolete!

She started off in life to be really independent. In that remote day, forty years ago, when a woman said she was going to be independent, it meant she was having no nonsense with men. She was kicking over the masculine traces, and living her own life, manless.

Today, when a girl says she is going to be independent, it means she is going to devote her attentions almost exclusively to men; though not necessarily to "a man."

Miss M'Leod had an income from her mother. Therefore, at the age of twenty, she turned her back on that image of tyranny, her father, and went to Paris to study art. Art having been studied, she turned her attention to the globe of earth. Being terribly independent, she soon made Africa look small; she dallied energetically with vast hinterlands of China; and she knew the Rocky Mountains and the deserts of Arizona as if she had been married to them. All this, to escape mere man.

The Lovely Lady

It was in New Mexico she purchased the blue moccasins, blue bead moccasins, from an Indian who was her guide and her subordinate. In her independence she made use of men, of course, but merely as servants, subordinates.

When the war broke out she came home. She was then forty-five, and already going grey. Her brother, two years older than herself, but a bachelor, went off to the war; she stayed at home in the small family mansion in the country, and did what she could. She was small and erect and brief in her speech, her face was like pale ivory, her skin like a very delicate parchment, and her eyes were very blue. There was no nonsense about her, though she did paint pictures. She never even touched her delicately parchment face with pigment. She was good enough as she was, honest-to-God, and the country town had a tremendous respect for her.

In her various activities she came pretty often into contact with Percy Barlow, the clerk at the bank. He was only twenty-two when she first set eyes on him, in 1914, and she immediately liked him. He was a stranger in the town, his father being a poor country vicar in Yorkshire. But he was of the confiding sort. He soon confided in Miss M'Leod, for whom he had a towering respect, how he disliked his step-mother, how he feared his father was but as wax in the hands of that downright woman, and how, in consequence, he was homeless. Wrath shone in his pleasant features, but somehow it was an amusing wrath; at least to Miss M'Leod.

The Blue Moccasins

He was distinctly a good-looking boy, with stiff dark hair and odd, twinkling grey eyes under thick dark brows, and a rather full mouth and a queer, deep voice that had a caressing touch of hoarseness. It was his voice that somehow got behind Miss M'Leod's reserve. Not that he had the faintest intention of so doing. He looked up to her immensely: "She's miles above me."

When she watched him playing tennis, letting himself go a bit too much, hitting too hard, running too fast, being too nice to his partner, her heart yearned over him. The orphan in him! Why should he go and be shot? She kept him at home as long as possible, working with her at all kinds of war-work. He was so absolutely willing to do everything she wanted: devoted to her.

But at last the time came when he must go. He was now twenty-four, and she forty-seven. He came to say good-bye, in his awkward fashion. She suddenly turned away, leaned her forehead against the wall, and burst into bitter tears. He was frightened out of his wits. Before he knew what was happening, he had his arm in front of his face and was sobbing, too.

She came to comfort him. "Don't cry, dear, don't! It will all be all right."

At last he wiped his face on his sleeve and looked at her sheepishly. "It was you crying as did me in," he said. Her blue eyes were brilliant with tears. She suddenly kissed him.

"You are such a dear!" she said wistfully. Then she added, flushing suddenly vivid pink under her transparent parchment skin: "It wouldn't be right for you to marry an old thing like me, would it?"

He looked at her dumbfounded.

"No, I'm too old," she added hastily.

"Don't talk about old! you're not old!" he said hotly.

"At least I'm too old for *that*," she said sadly.

"Not as far as I'm concerned," he said. "You're younger than me, in most ways, I'm hanged if you're not!"

"Are you hanged if I'm not?" she teased wistfully.

"I am," he said. "And if I thought you wanted me, I'd be jolly proud if you married me. I would, I assure you."

"Would you?" she said, still teasing him.

Nevertheless, the next time he was home on leave she married him, very quietly, but very definitely. He was a young lieutenant. They stayed in her family home, Twybit Hall, for the honeymoon. It was her house now, her brother being dead. And they had a strangely happy month. She had made a strange discovery: a man.

He went off to Gallipoli, and became a captain. He came home in 1919, still green with malaria, but otherwise sound. She was in her fiftieth year. And she was almost white-haired; long, thick white hair, done perfectly, and perfectly creamy, colourless face, with very blue eyes.

He had been true to her, not being very forward with women. But he was a bit startled by her white

The Blue Moccasins

hair. However, he shut his eyes to it, and loved her. And she, though frightened and somewhat bewildered, was happy. But she was bewildered. It always seemed awkward to her, that he should come wandering into her room in his pyjamas when she was half dressed, and brushing her hair. And he would sit there silent, watching her brush the long swinging river of silver, of her white hair, the bare, ivory-white slender arm working with a strange mechanical motion, sharp and forcible, brushing down the long silvery stream of hair. He would sit as if mesmerized, just gazing. And she would at last glance round sharply, and he would rise, saying some little casual thing to her and smiling to her oddly with his eyes. Then he would go out, his thin cotton pyjamas hitching up over his hips, for he was a rather big-built fellow. And she would feel dazed, as if she did not quite know her own self any more. And the queer, ducking motion of his silently going out of her door impressed her ominously, his curious cat head, his big hips and limbs.

They were alone in the house, save for the servants. He had no work. They lived modestly, for a good deal of her money had been lost during the war. But she still painted pictures. Marriage had only stimulated her to this. She painted canvases of flowers, beautiful flowers that thrilled her soul. And he would sit, pipe in fist, silent, and watch her. He had nothing to do. He just sat and watched her small, neat figure and her concentrated movements, as she painted. Then he knocked out his pipe, and filled it again.

The Lovely Lady

She said that at last she was perfectly happy. And he said that he was perfectly happy. They were always together. He hardly went out, save riding in the lanes. And practically nobody came to the house.

But still, they were very silent with one another. The old chatter had died out. And he did not read much. He just sat still, and smoked, and was silent. It got on her nerves sometimes, and she would think, as she had thought in the past, that the highest bliss a human being can experience is perhaps the bliss of being quite alone, quite, quite alone.

His bank firm offered to make him manager of the local branch, and, at her advice, he accepted. Now he went out of the house every morning and came home every evening, which was much more agreeable. The rector begged him to sing again in the church choir, and again she advised him to accept. These were the old grooves in which his bachelor life had run. He felt more like himself.

He was popular: a nice, harmless fellow, everyone said of him. Some of the men secretly pitied him. They made rather much of him, took him home to luncheon, and let him loose with their daughters. He was popular among the daughters, too: naturally, for, if a girl expressed a wish, he would instinctively say: "What! would you like it? I'll get it for you." And if he were not in a position to satisfy the desire, he would say: "I only wish I could do it for you. I'd do it like a shot." All of which he meant.

At the same time, though he got on so well with the

maidens of the town, there was no coming forward about him. He was, in some way, not wakened up. Good-looking, and big, and serviceable, he was inwardly remote, without self-confidence, almost without a self at all.

The rector's daughter took it upon herself to wake him up. She was exactly as old as he was, a smallish, rather sharp-faced young woman who had lost her husband in the war, and it had been a grief to her. But she took the stoic attitude of the young: You've got to live, so you may as well do it!—She was a kindly soul, in spite of her sharpness. And she had a very perky little red-brown pomeranian dog that she had bought in Florence in the street, but which had turned out a handsome little fellow. Miss M'Leod looked down a bit on Alice Howells and her pom, so Mrs. Howells felt no special love for Miss M'Leod—"Mrs. Barlow, that is!" she would add sharply. "For it's quite impossible to think of her as anything but Miss M'Leod!"

Percy was really more at ease at the rectory, where the pom yapped and Mrs. Howells changed her dress three or four times a day and looked it, than in the semi-cloistral atmosphere of Twybit Hall, where Miss M'Leod wore tweeds and a natural knitted jumper, her skirts rather long, her hair done up pure silver, and painted her wonderful flower pictures in the deepening silence of the daytime. At evening she would go up to change, after he came home. And though it thrilled her to have a man coming into her room as he dressed, snapping his collar-stud, to tell her something trivial as she stood bare-armed in her silk slip, rapidly coiling up the rope of silver hair behind her head, still, it worried her. When he was there, he couldn't keep away from her. And he would watch her, watch her, watch her as if she was the ultimate revelation. Sometimes it made her irritable. She was so absolutely used to her own privacy. What was he looking at? She never watched *him*. Rather she looked the other way. His watching tried her nerves. She was turned fifty. And his great silent body loomed almost dreadful.

He was quite happy playing tennis or croquet with Alice Howells and the rest. Alice was choir-mistress, a bossy little person outwardly, inwardly rather forlorn and affectionate, and not very sure that life hadn't let her down for good. She was now over thirty—and had no one but the pom and her father and the parish—nothing in her really intimate life. But she was very cheerful, busy, even gay, with her choir and school work, her dancing and flirting and dressmaking.

She was intrigued by Percy Barlow. "How *can* a man be so nice to *everybody*?" she asked him, a little exasperated. "Well, why not?" he replied, with the odd smile of his eyes. "It's not why he shouldn't, but how he manages to do it! How can you have so much good-nature? I *have* to be catty to some people, but you're nice to *everybody*."

"Oh, am I!" he said ominously.

He was like a man in a dream, or in a cloud. He was quite a good bank-manager, in fact very intelligent. Even in appearance, his great charm was his beautifully shaped head. He had plenty of brains, really. But in his will, in his body, he was asleep. And sometimes this lethargy, or coma, made him look haggard. And sometimes it made his body seem inert and despicable, meaningless.

Alice Howells longed to ask him about his wife. "*Do* you love her? *Can* you really care for her?" But she daren't. She daren't ask him one word about his wife. Another thing she couldn't do, she couldn't persuade him to dance. Never, not once. But in everything else he was pliable as wax.

Mrs. Barlow—Miss M'Leod—stayed out at Twybit all the time. She did not even come in to church on Sunday. She had shaken off church, among other things. And she watched Percy depart, and felt just a little humiliated. He was going to sing in the choir! Yes, marriage was also a humiliation to her. She had distinctly married beneath her.

The years had gone by: she was now fifty-seven, Percy was thirty-four. He was still, in many ways, a boy. But in his curious silence, he was ageless. She managed him with perfect ease. If she expressed a wish, he acquiesced at once. So now it was agreed he should not come to her room any more. And he never did. But sometimes she went to him in his room, and was winsome in a pathetic, heart-breaking way.

She twisted him round her little finger, as the saying goes. And yet secretly she was afraid of him. In the early years he had displayed a clumsy but violent sort of passion, from which she had shrunk away. She felt it had nothing to do with her. It was just his indis-criminating desire for Woman, and for his own satis-faction. Whereas she was not just unidentified Woman, to give him his general satisfaction. So she had recoiled, and withdrawn herself. She had put him off. She had regained the absolute privacy of her room.

He was perfectly sweet about it. Yet she was uneasy with him now. She was afraid of him; or rather, not of him, but of a mysterious something in him. She was not a bit afraid of *him*, oh no! And when she went to him now, to be nice to him, in her pathetic winsome-ness of an unused woman of fifty-seven, she found him sweet-natured as ever, but really indifferent. He saw her pathos and her winsomeness. In some way, the mystery of her, her thick white hair, her vivid blue eyes, her ladylike refinement still fascinated him. But his bodily desire for her had gone, utterly gone. And secretly, she was rather glad. But as he looked at her, looked at her, as he lay there so silent, she was afraid, as if some finger were pointed at her. Yet she knew, the moment she spoke to him, he would twist his eyes to that good-natured and "kindly" smile of his.

It was in the late, dark months of this year that she missed the blue moccasins. She had hung them on a nail in his room. Not that he ever wore them: they were too small. Nor did she: they were too big. Moc-casins are male footwear, among the Indians, not fe-male. But they were of a lovely turquoise-blue colour, made all of little turquoise beads, with little forked flames of dead-white and dark-green. When, at the beginning of their marriage, he had exclaimed over them, she had said: "Yes! Aren't they a lovely colour! so blue!" And he had replied: "Not as blue as your eyes, even then."

So naturally, she had hung them up on the wall in his room, and there they had stayed. Till, one November day, when there were no flowers, and she was pining to paint a still-life with something blue in it—oh, so blue, like delphiniums!—she had gone to his room for the moccasins. And they were not there. And though she hunted, she could not find them. Nor did the maids know anything of them.

So she asked him: "Percy, do you know where those blue moccasins are, which hung in your room?"— There was a moment's dead silence. Then he looked at her with his good-naturedly twinkling eyes, and said: "No, *I* know nothing of them."—There was another dead pause. She did not believe him. But being a perfect lady, she only said, as she turned away: "Well then, how curious it is!"—And there was another dead pause. Out of which he asked her what she wanted them for, and she told him. Whereon the matter lapsed.

It was November, and Percy was out in the evening fairly often now. He was rehearsing for a "play" which was to be given in the church schoolroom at Christmas. He had asked her about it. "Do you think it's a bit *infra dig.* if I play one of the characters?" She had looked at him mildly, disguising her real feeling. "If you don't feel *personally* humiliated," she said, "then there's nothing else to consider." And he had answered: "Oh, it doesn't upset *me* at all." So she mildly said: "Then do it, by all means." Adding at the back of her mind: If it amuses you, child!—But, she thought, a change had indeed come over the world, when the master of Twybit Hall, or even, for that matter, the manager of the dignified Stubbs's Bank, should perform in public on a schoolroom stage in amateur theatricals. And she kept calmly aloof, preferring not to know any details. She had a world of her own.

When he had said to Alice Howells: "You don't think other folk'll mind?—clients of the bank and so forth—think it beneath my dignity?" she had cried, looking up into his twinkling eyes: "Oh, you don't have to keep *your* dignity on ice, Percy—any more than I do mine."

The play was to be performed for the first time on Christmas Eve; and after the play there was the midnight service in church. Percy therefore told his wife not to expect him home till the small hours, at least. So he drove himself off in the car.

As night fell, and rain, Miss M'Leod felt a little forlorn. She was left out of everything. Life was slipping past her. It was Christmas Eve, and she was more alone than she had ever been. Percy only seemed to intensify her aloneness, leaving her in this fashion.

She decided not to be left out. She would go to the play, too. It was past six o'clock, and she had worked herself into a highly nervous state. Outside was darkness and rain; inside was silence, forlornness. She went to the telephone and rang up the garage in Shewbury. It was with great difficulty she got them to promise to send a car for her: Mr. Slater would have to fetch her himself in the two-seater runabout; everything else was out.

She dressed nervously, in a dark green dress with a few modest jewels. Looking at herself in the mirror, she still thought herself slim, young-looking, and distinguished. She did not see how old-fashioned she was, with her uncompromising erectness, her glistening knob of silver hair sticking out behind, and her long dress.

It was a three-mile drive in the rain, to the small country town. She sat next to old Slater, who was used to driving horses and was nervous and clumsy with a car, without saying a word. He thankfully deposited her at the gate of St. Barnabas's School.

It was almost half-past seven. The schoolroom was packed and buzzing with excitement. "I'm afraid we haven't a seat left, Mrs. Barlow!" said Jackson, one of the church sidesmen, who was standing guard in the school porch, where people were still fighting to get in. He faced her in consternation. She faced him in consternation.—"Well, I shall have to stay somewhere, till Mr. Barlow can drive me home," she said. "Couldn't you put me a chair somewhere?"

Worried and flustered, he went worrying and flustering the other people in charge. The schoolroom was simply packed solid. But Mr. Simmons, the leading grocer, gave up his chair in the front row to Mrs. Barlow, whilst he sat in a chair right under the stage, where he couldn't see a thing. But he could see Mrs. Barlow seated between his wife and daughter, speaking a word or two to them occasionally, and that was enough.

The lights went down; *The Shoes of Shagput* was about to begin. The amateur curtains were drawn back, disclosing the little amateur stage with a white amateur back-cloth daubed to represent a Moorish courtyard. In stalked Percy, dressed as a Moor, his face darkened. He looked quite handsome, his pale grey eyes queer and startling in his dark face. But he was afraid of the audience—he spoke away from them, stalking around clumsily. After a certain amount of would-be funny dialogue, in tripped the heroine, Alice Howells, of course. She was an eastern Houri, in white gauze Turkish trousers, silver veil, and—the blue moccasins. The whole stage was white, save for her blue moccasins, Percy's dark-green sash, and a Negro boy's red fez.

When Mrs. Barlow saw the blue moccasins, a little bomb of rage exploded in her. This, of all places! the blue moccasins that she had bought in the western deserts! the blue moccasins that were not so blue as her own eyes! *Her* blue moccasins! on the feet of that creature, Mrs. Howells.

Alice Howells was not afraid of the audience. She looked full at them, lifting her silver veil. And, of course, she saw Mrs. Barlow, sitting there like the Ancient of Days in judgment, in the front row. And a bomb of rage exploded in *her* breast, too.

In the play, Alice was the wife of the grey-bearded old Caliph, but she captured the love of the young Ali, otherwise Percy, and the whole business was the attempt of these two to evade Caliph and Negro-eunuchs and ancient crones, and get into each other's arms. The blue shoes were very important; for, while the secret Leila wore them, the gallant Ali was to know there was danger. But when she took them off, he might approach her.

It was all quite childish, and everybody loved it, and Miss M'Leod might have been quite complacent about it all, had not Alice Howells got her monkey up, so to speak. Alice, with a lot of make-up, looked boldly handsome. And suddenly bold she was, bold as the devil. All these years the poor young widow had been "good," slaving in the parish, and only even flirting just to cheer things up, never going very far and knowing she could never get anything out of it, but determined never to mope.

Now the sight of Miss M'Leod sitting there so erect, so coolly "higher plane," and calmly superior, suddenly let loose a devil in Alice Howells. All her limbs went suave and molten, as her young sex, long pent up, flooded even to her finger-tips. Her voice was strange, even to herself, with its long, plaintive notes. She felt all her movements soft and fluid, she felt herself like living liquid. And it was lovely. Underneath it all was the sting of malice against Miss M'Leod, sitting there so erect, with her great knob of white hair.

Alice's business, as the lovely Leila, was to be seductive to the rather heavy Percy. And seductive she was. In two minutes, she had him spellbound. He saw nothing of the audience. A faint, fascinated grin came on to his face, as he acted up to the young woman in the Turkish trousers. His rather full, coarse voice changed and became clear, with a new, naked clang in it. When the two sang together, in the simple banal duets of the play, it was with a most fascinating intimacy. And when, at the end of Act one, the lovely Leila kicked off the blue moccasins, saying: "Away, shoes of bondage, shoes of sorrow!" and danced a little dance all alone, barefoot, in her Turkish trousers, in front of her fascinated hero, his smile was so spellbound that everybody else was spellbound, too.

Miss M'Leod's indignation knew no bounds. When the blue moccasins were kicked across the stage by the brazen Alice, with the words: "Away, shoes of bondage, shoes of sorrow!" the elder woman grew pink with fury, and it was all she could do not to rise and snatch the moccasins from the stage, and bear them away. She sat in speechless indignation during the brief curtain between Act one and Act two. Her moccasins! her blue moccasins! of the sacred blue colour, the turquoise of heaven.

But there they were, in Act two, on the feet of the bold Alice. It was becoming too much. And the love-scenes between Percy and the young woman were becoming nakedly shameful. Alice grew worse and worse. She was worked up now, caught in her own spell, and unconscious of everything save of him, and the sting of that other woman, who presumed to own him. Own him? Ha-ha!—For he was fascinated. The queer smile on his face, the concentrated gleam of his eyes, the queer way he leant forward from his loins towards her, the new, reckless, throaty twang in his voice—the audience had before their eyes a man spell-bound and lost in passion.

Miss M'Leod sat in shame and torment, as if her chair was red-hot. She too was fast losing her normal consciousness, in the spell of rage. She was outraged. The second Act was working to its climax. The climax came. The lovely Leila kicked off the blue shoes: "Away, shoes of bondage, away!" and flew barefoot to the enraptured Ali, flinging herself into his arms. And if ever a man was gone in sheer desire, it was Percy, as he pressed the woman's lithe form against his body, and seemed unconsciously to envelop her, unaware of everything else. While she, blissful in his spell, but still aware of the audience and of the superior Miss M'Leod, let herself be wrapped closer and closer.

Miss M'Leod rose to her feet and looked towards the door. But the way out was packed with people standing holding their breath as the two on the stage remained wrapped in each other's arms, and the three fiddles and the flute softly woke up. Miss M'Leod could not bear it. She was on her feet, and beside herself. She could not get out. She could not sit down again.

"Percy!" she said, in a low clear voice. "Will you hand me my moccasins?"

He lifted his face like a man startled in a dream, lifted his face from the shoulder of his Leila. His gold-grey eyes were like softly startled flames. He looked in sheer horrified wonder at the little white-haired woman standing below.

"Eh?" he said, purely dazed.

"Will you please hand me my moccasins?"—and she pointed to where they lay on the stage.

Alice had stepped away from him, and was gazing at the risen viper of the little elderly woman on the tip of the audience. Then she watched him move across the stage, bending forward from the loins in his queer mesmerized way, pick up the blue moccasins, and stoop down to hand them over the edge of the stage to his wife, who reached up for them.

"Thank you!" said Miss M'Leod, seating herself, with the blue moccasins in her lap.

Alice recovered her composure, gave a sign to the little orchestra, and began to sing at once, strong and assured, to sing her part in the duet that closed the Act. She knew she could command public opinion in her favour.

He, too, recovered at once, the little smile came back on his face, he calmly forgot his wife again as he sang his share in the duet. It was finished. The curtains were pulled to. There was immense cheering. The

The Blue Moccasins

curtains opened, and Alice and Percy bowed to the audience, smiling both of them their peculiar secret smile, while Miss M'Leod sat with the blue moccasins on her lap.

The curtains were closed, it was the long interval. After a few moments of hesitation, Mrs. Barlow rose with dignity, gathered her wrap over her arm, and, with the blue moccasins in her hand, moved towards the door. Way was respectfully made for her.

"I should like to speak to Mr. Barlow," she said to Jackson, who had anxiously ushered her in, and now would anxiously usher her out.

"Yes, Mrs. Barlow."

He led her round to the smaller classroom at the back, that acted as dressing-room. The amateur actors were drinking lemonade, and chattering freely. Mrs. Howells came forward, and Jackson whispered the news to her. She turned to Percy.

"Percy, Mrs. Barlow wants to speak to you. Shall I come with you?"

"Speak to me? Aye, come on with me."

The two followed the anxious Jackson into the other half-lighted classroom, where Mrs. Barlow stood in her wrap, holding the moccasins. She was very pale, and she watched the two butter-muslin Turkish figures enter as if they could not possibly be real. She ignored Mrs. Howells entirely.

"Percy," she said, "I want you to drive me home."

"Drive you home?" he echoed.

"Yes, please!"

"Why—when?" he said, with vague bluntness.

"Now—if you don't mind——"

"What—in this get-up?" He looked at himself.

"I could wait while you changed."

There was a pause. He turned and looked at Alice Howells, and Alice Howells looked at him. The two women saw each other out of the corners of their eyes; but it was beneath notice. He turned to his wife, his black face ludicrously blank, his eyebrows cocked.

"Well, you see," he said, "it's rather awkward. I can hardly hold up the third Act while I've taken you home and got back here again, can I?"

"So you intend to play in the third Act?" she asked with cold ferocity.

"Why, I must, mustn't I?" he said blankly.

"Do you *wish* to?" she said, in all her intensity.

"I do, naturally. I want to finish the thing up properly," he replied, in the utter innocence of his head; about his heart he knew nothing.

She turned sharply away.

"Very well!" she said. And she called to Jackson, who was standing dejectedly by the door: "Mr. Jackson, will you please find some car or conveyance to take me home?"

"Aye!—I say, Mr. Jackson," called Percy in his strong, democratic voice, going forward to the man. "Ask Tom Lomas if he'll do me a good turn and get my car out of the rectory garage, to drive Mrs. Barlow home.—Aye, ask Tom Lomas! And if not him, ask

The Blue Moccasins

Mr. Pilkington—Leonard. The key's there. You don't mind, do you?—I'm ever so much obliged. . . ."

The three were left awkwardly alone again.

"I expect you've had enough with two acts," said Percy soothingly to his wife. "These things aren't up to your mark. I know it. They're only child's play. But, you see, they please the people. We've got a packed house, haven't we?"

His wife had nothing to answer. He looked so ludicrous, with his dark brown face and butter-muslin bloomers. And his mind was so ludicrously innocent. His body, however, was not so ridiculously innocent as his mind, as she knew when he turned to the other woman.

"You and I, we're more on the nonsense level, aren't we?" he said, with the new, throaty clang of naked intimacy in his voice. His wife shivered.

"Absolutely on the nonsense level," said Alice, with easy assurance.

She looked into his eyes, then she looked at the blue moccasins in the hand of the other woman. He gave a little start, as if realizing something for himself.

At that moment Tom Lomas looked in, saying heartily: "Right you are, Percy! I'll have my car here in half a tick. I'm more handy with it than yours."

"Thanks, old man! You're a Christian."

"Try to be!—especially when you turn Turk! Well . . ." He disappeared.

"I say, Lina," said Percy in his most amiable demo-

cratic way, "would you mind leaving the moccasins
for the next act? We s'll be in a bit of a hole without
them."

Miss M'Leod faced him and stared at him with the
full blast of her forget-me-not blue eyes, from her
white face.

"Will you pardon me if I don't?" she said.

"What!" he exclaimed. "Why? Why not? It's
nothing but play, to amuse the people. I can't see how
it can hurt the *moccasins*. I understand you don't quite
like seeing me make a fool of myself. But anyhow, I'm
a bit of a born fool. What?"—and his blackened face
laughed with a Turkish laugh. "Oh, yes, you have to
realize I rather enjoy playing the fool," he resumed.
"And, after all, it doesn't really hurt *you*, now does it?
Shan't you leave us those moccasins for the last act?"

She looked at him, then at the moccasins in her hand.
No, it was useless to yield to so ludicrous a person. The
vulgarity of his wheedling, the commonness of the
whole performance! It was useless to yield even the
moccasins. It would be treachery to herself.

"I'm sorry," she said. "But I'd so much rather they
weren't used for this kind of thing. I never intended
them to be." She stood with her face averted from the
ridiculous couple.

He changed as if she had slapped his face. He sat
down on top of the low pupils' desk, and gazed with
glazed interest round the classroom. Alice sat beside
him, in her white gauze and her bedizened face. They

The Blue Moccasins

were like two rebuked sparrows on one twig, he with his great, easy, intimate limbs, she so light and alert. And as he sat he sank into an unconscious physical sympathy with her. Miss M'Leod walked towards the door.

"You'll have to think of something as'll do instead," he muttered to Alice in a low voice, meaning the blue moccasins. And leaning down, he drew off one of the grey shoes she had on, caressing her foot with the slip of his hand over its slim bare shape. She hastily put the bare foot behind her other, shod foot.

Tom Lomas poked in his head, his overcoat collar turned up to his ears.

"Car's there," he said.

"Right-o, Tom! I'll chalk it up to thee, lad!" said Percy with heavy breeziness. Then, making a great effort with himself, he rose heavily and went across to the door, to his wife, saying to her, in the same stiff voice of false heartiness:

"You'll be as right as rain with Tom. You won't mind if I don't come out? No! I'd better not show myself to the audience. Well—I'm glad you came, if only for a while. Good-bye, then! I'll be home after the service—but I shan't disturb you. Good-bye! Don't get wet now. . . ." And his voice, falsely cheerful, stiff with anger, ended in a clang of indignation.

Alice Howells sat on the infants' bench in silence. She was ignored. And she was unhappy, uneasy, because of the scene.

Percy closed the door after his wife. Then he turned

141

with a looming slowness to Alice, and said in a hoarse whisper: "Think o' that, now!"

She looked up at him anxiously. His face, in its dark pigment, was transfigured with indignant anger. His yellow-grey eyes blazed, and a great rush of anger seemed to be surging up volcanic in him. For a second his eyes rested on her upturned, troubled dark blue eyes, then glanced away, as if he didn't want to look at her in his anger. Even so, she felt a touch of tenderness in his glance.

"And that's all she's ever cared about—her own things and her own way," he said, in the same hoarse whisper, hoarse with suddenly released rage. Alice Howells hung her head in silence.

"Not another damned thing, but what's her own, her own—and her own holy way—damned holy-holy-holy, all to herself." His voice shook with hoarse, whispering rage, burst out at last.

Alice Howells looked up at him in distress.

"Oh, don't say it!" she said. "I'm sure she's fond of you."

"*Fond* of me! Fond of *me*!" he blazed, with a grin of transcendent irony. "It makes her sick to look at me. I am a hairy brute, I own it.—Why, she's never once touched me to be fond of me—never once—though she pretends sometimes. But a man knows—" and he made a grimace of contempt. "He knows when a woman's just stroking him, good doggie!—and when she's really a bit woman-fond of him.—That woman's never been real fond of anybody or anything, all her life—she couldn't, for all her show of kindness. She's limited to herself, that woman is; and I've looked up to her as if she was God. More fool me! If God's not good-natured and good-hearted, then what is He . . . ?"

Alice sat with her head dropped, realizing once more that men aren't really fooled. She was upset, shaken by his rage, and frightened, as if she too were guilty. He had sat down blankly beside her. She glanced up at him.

"Never mind!" she said soothingly. "You'll like her again tomorrow."

He looked down at her with a grin, a grey sort of grin.—"Are you going to stroke me good doggie! as well?" he said.

"Why?" she asked, blank.

But he did not answer. Then after a while he resumed: "Wouldn't even leave the moccasins! And she'd hung them up in my room, left them there for years—any man'd consider they were his.—And I did want this show tonight to be a success!—What are you going to do about it?"

"I've sent over for a pair of pale blue satin bedslippers of mine—they'll do just as well," she replied.

"Aye!—For all that, it's done me in."

"You'll get over it."

"Happen so! She's curdled my inside, for all that. I don't know how I'm going to be civil to her."

"Perhaps you'd better stay at the rectory tonight," she said softly.

The Lovely Lady

He looked into her eyes. And in that look, he transferred his allegiance.

"*You* don't want to be drawn in, do you?" he asked, with troubled tenderness.

But she only gazed with wide, darkened eyes into his eyes, so she was like an open, dark doorway to him. His heart beat thick, and the faint, breathless smile of passion came into his eyes again.

"You'll have to go on, Mrs. Howells. We can't keep them waiting any longer."

It was Jim Stokes, who was directing the show. They heard the clapping and stamping of the impatient audience.

"Goodness!" cried Alice Howells, darting to the door.

Things

They were true idealists, from New England. But that is some time ago: before the war. Several years before the war, they met and married; he a tall, keen-eyed young man from Connecticut, she a smallish, demure, Puritan-looking young woman from Massachusetts. They both had a little money. Not much, however. Even added together, it didn't make three thousand dollars a year. Still—they were free. Free!

Ah!—freedom! To be free to live one's own life! To be twenty-five and twenty-seven, a pair of true idealists with a mutual love of beauty, and an inclination towards "Indian thought"—meaning, alas, Mrs. Besant—and an income a little under three thousand dollars a year! But what is money? All one wishes to do is to live a full and beautiful life. In Europe, of course, right at the fountain-head of tradition. It might possibly be done in America; in New England, for example. But at a forfeiture of a certain amount of "beauty." True beauty takes a long time to mature. The baroque is only half beautiful, half matured. No, the real silver bloom, the real golden-sweet bouquet of beauty had its roots in the Renaissance, not in any later or shallower period.

147

The Lovely Lady

Therefore the two idealists, who were married in New Haven, sailed at once to Paris: Paris of the old days. They had a studio apartment on the Boulevard Montparnasse, and they became real Parisians, in the old, delightful sense, not in the modern, vulgar. It was the shimmer of the pure impressionists, Monet and his followers, the world seen in terms of pure light, light broken and unbroken. How lovely! How lovely the nights, the river, the mornings in the old streets and by the flower-stalls and the book-stalls, the afternoons up on Montmartre or in the Tuileries, the evenings on the boulevards!

They both painted, but not desperately. Art had not taken them by the throat, and they did not take Art by the throat. They painted: that's all. They knew people—nice people, if possible, though one had to take them mixed. And they were happy.

Yet it seems as if human beings must set their claws in *something*. To be "free," to be "living a full and beautiful life," you must, alas, be attached to something. A "full and beautiful life" means a tight attachment to *something*—at least, it is so for all idealists —or else a certain boredom supervenes; there is a certain waving of loose ends upon the air, like the waving, yearning tendrils of the vine that spread and rotate, seeking something to clutch, something up which to climb towards the necessary sun. Finding nothing, the vine can only trail, half fulfilled, upon the ground. Such is freedom!—a clutching of the right pole. And human beings are all vines. But especially the idealist.

Things

He is a vine, and he needs to clutch and climb. And he despises the man who is a mere *potato*, or turnip, or lump of wood.

Our idealists were frightfully happy, but they were all the time reaching out for something to cotton on to. At first, Paris was enough. They explored Paris *thoroughly*. And they learned French till they almost felt like French people, they could speak it so glibly.

Still, you know, you never talk French with your *soul*. It can't be done. And though it's very thrilling, at first, talking in French to clever Frenchmen—they seem *so* much cleverer than oneself—still, in the long run, it is not satisfying. The endlessly clever *materialism* of the French leaves you cold in the end, gives a sense of barrenness and incompatibility with true New England depth. So our two idealists felt.

They turned away from France—but ever so gently. France had disappointed them. "We've loved it, and we've got a great deal out of it. But after a while, after a considerable while, several years, in fact, Paris leaves one feeling disappointed. It hasn't quite got what one wants."

"But Paris isn't France."

"No, perhaps not. France is quite different from Paris. And France is lovely—quite lovely. But *to us*, though we love it, it doesn't say a great deal."

So, when the war came, the idealists moved to Italy. And they loved Italy. They found it beautiful, and more poignant than France. It seemed much nearer to the New England conception of beauty: something pure, and full of sympathy, without the *materialism* and the *cynicism* of the French. The two idealists seemed to breathe their own true air in Italy.

And in Italy, much more than in Paris, they felt they could thrill to the teachings of the Buddha. They entered the swelling stream of modern Buddhistic emotion, and they read the books, and they practised meditation, and they deliberately set themselves to eliminate from their own souls greed, pain, and sorrow. They did not realize—yet—that Buddha's very eagerness to free himself from pain and sorrow is in itself a sort of greed. No, they dreamed of a perfect world, from which all greed, and nearly all pain, and a great deal of sorrow, were eliminated.

But America entered the war, so the two idealists had to help. They did hospital work. And though their experience made them realize more than ever that greed, pain, and sorrow *should* be eliminated from the world, nevertheless the Buddhism, or the theosophy, didn't emerge very triumphant from the long crisis. Somehow, somewhere, in some part of themselves, they felt that greed, pain, and sorrow would never be eliminated, because most people don't care about eliminating them, and never will care. Our idealists were far too western to think of abandoning all the world to damnation, while they saved their two selves. They were far too unselfish to sit tight under a bho tree and reach Nirvana in a mere couple.

It was more than that, though. They simply hadn't enough *Sitzfleisch* to squat under a bho tree and get to Nirvana by contemplating anything, least of all their own navel. If the whole wide world was not going to be saved, they, personally, were not so very keen on being saved just by themselves. No, it would be so lonesome. They were New Englanders, so it must be all or nothing. Greed, pain, and sorrow must either be eliminated from *all the world*, or else, what was the use of eliminating them from oneself? No use at all! One was just a victim.

And so, although they still *loved* "Indian thought," and felt very tender about it: well, to go back to our metaphor, the pole up which the green and anxious vines had clambered so far now proved dry-rotten. It snapped, and the vines came slowly subsiding to earth again. There was no crack and crash. The vines held themselves up by their own foliage, for a while. But they subsided. The beanstalk of "Indian thought" had given way before Jack and Jill had climbed off the tip of it to a further world.

They subsided with a slow rustle back to earth again. But they made no outcry. They were again "disappointed." But they never admitted it. "Indian thought" had let them down. But they never complained. Even to one another, they never said a word. They were disappointed, faintly but deeply disillusioned, and they both knew it. But the knowledge was tacit.

And they still had so much in their lives. They still had Italy—dear Italy. And they still had freedom, the priceless treasure. And they still had so much "beauty." About the fullness of their lives they were not quite so sure. They had one little boy, whom they loved as parents should love their children, but whom they wisely refrained from fastening upon, to build their lives on him. No, no, they must live their own lives! They still had strength of mind to know that.

But they were now no longer so very young. Twenty-five and twenty-seven had become thirty-five and thirty-seven. And though they had had a very wonderful time in Europe, and though they still loved Italy—dear Italy!—yet: they were disappointed. They had got a lot out of it; oh, a very great deal indeed! Still, it hadn't given them quite, not *quite*, what they had expected. Europe was lovely, but it was dead. Living in Europe, you were living on the past. And Europeans, with all their superficial charm, were not *really* charming. They were materialistic, they had no *real* soul. They just did not understand the inner urge of the spirit, because the inner urge was dead in them, they were all survivals. There, that was the truth about Europeans: they were survivals, with no more getting ahead in them.

It was another bean-pole, another vine-support crumbled under the green life of the vine. And very bitter it was, this time. For up the old tree-trunk of Europe the green vine had been clambering silently for more than ten years, ten hugely important years, the years of real living. The two idealists had *lived* in Europe, lived on Europe and on European life and European things as vines in an everlasting vineyard.

They had made their home here: a home such as

Things

you could never make in America. Their watchword
had been "beauty." They had rented, the last four
years, the second floor of an old Palazzo on the Arno,
and here they had all their "things." And they derived
a profound, profound satisfaction from their apartment: the lofty, silent, ancient rooms with windows
on the river, with glistening, dark red floors, and the
beautiful furniture that the idealists had "picked up."

Yes, unknown to themselves, the lives of the idealists
had been running with a fierce swiftness horizontally,
all the time. They had become tense, fierce hunters of
"things" for their home. While their souls were
climbing up to the sun of old European culture or old
Indian thought, their passions were running horizontally, clutching at "things." Of course, they did not
buy the things for the things' sakes, but for the sake
of "beauty." They looked upon their home as a place
entirely furnished by loveliness, not by "things" at
all. Valerie had some very lovely curtains at the
windows of the long *salotta*, looking on the river: curtains of queer ancient material that looked like finely
knitted silk, most beautifully faded down from ver-
milion and orange and gold and black, down to a sheer
soft glow. Valerie hardly ever came into the *salotta*
without mentally falling on her knees before the curtains. "Chartres!" she said. "To me they are Chartres!"
And Melville never turned and looked at his sixteenth-
century Venetian bookcase, with its two or three
dozen of choice books, without feeling his marrow stir
in his bones. The holy of holies!

The Lovely Lady

The child silently, almost sinisterly, avoided any rude contact with these ancient monuments of furniture, as if they had been nests of sleeping cobras, or that "thing" most perilous to the touch, the Ark of the Covenant. His childish awe was silent and cold, but final.

Still, a couple of New England idealists cannot live merely on the bygone glory of their furniture. At least, one couple could not. They got used to the marvellous Bologna cupboard, they got used to the wonderful Venetian bookcase, and the books, and the Siena curtains and bronzes, and the lovely sofas and side-tables and chairs they had "picked up" in Paris. Oh, they had been picking things up since the first day they landed in Europe. And they were still at it. It is the last interest Europe can offer to an outsider; or to an insider either.

When people came, and were thrilled by the Melville interior, then Valerie and Erasmus felt they had not lived in vain, that they still were living. But in the long mornings, when Erasmus was desultorily working at Renaissance Florentine literature, and Valerie was attending to the apartment, and in the long hours after lunch, and in the long, usually very cold and oppressive evenings in the ancient palazzo, then the halo died from around the furniture, and the things became things, lumps of matter that just stood there or hung there, *ad infinitum*, and said nothing; and Valerie and Erasmus almost hated them. The glow of beauty, like every other glow, dies down unless it is fed. The

Things

idealists still dearly loved their things. But they had got them. And the sad fact is, things that glow vividly while you're getting them go almost quite cold after a year or two. Unless, of course, people envy them very much, and the museums are pining for them. And the Melvilles' "things," though very good, were not quite so good as that.

So, the glow gradually went out of everything, out of Europe, out of Italy—"the Italians are *dears*"—even out of that marvellous apartment on the Arno. "Why, if I had this apartment, I'd never, never even want to go out of doors! It's too lovely and perfect." That was something, of course—to hear that.

And yet Valerie and Erasmus went out of doors; they even went out to get away from its ancient, cold-floored, stone-heavy silence and dead dignity. "We're living on the past, you know, Dick," said Valerie to her husband. She called him Dick.

They were grimly hanging on. They did not like to give in. They did not like to own up that they were through. For twelve years, now, they had been "free" people living a "full and beautiful life." And America for twelve years had been their anathema, the Sodom and Gomorrah of industrial materialism.

It wasn't easy to own that you were "through." They hated to admit that they wanted to go back. But at last, reluctantly, they decided to go, "for the boy's sake."—"We can't *bear* to leave Europe. But Peter is an American, so he had better look at America while he's young."—The Melvilles had an entirely English

155

accent and manner; almost; a little Italian and French here and there.

They left Europe behind, but they took as much of it along with them as possible. Several van-loads, as a matter of fact. All those adorable and irreplaceable "things." And all arrived in New York, idealists, child, and the huge bulk of Europe they had lugged along.

Valerie had dreamed of a pleasant apartment, perhaps on Riverside Drive, where it was not so expensive as east of Fifth Avenue, and where all their wonderful things would look marvellous. She and Erasmus house-hunted. But alas! their income was quite under three thousand dollars a year. They found—well, everybody knows what they found. Two small rooms and a kitchenette, and don't let us unpack a *thing*!

The chunk of Europe which they had bitten off went into a warehouse, at fifty dollars a month. And they sat in two small rooms and a kitchenette, and wondered why they'd done it.

Erasmus, of course, ought to get a job. This was what was written on the wall, and what they both pretended not to see. But it had been the strange, vague threat that the Statue of Liberty had always held over them: "Thou shalt get a job!" Erasmus had the tickets, as they say. A scholastic career was still possible for him. He had taken his exams brilliantly at Yale, and had kept up his "researches," all the time he had been in Europe.

But both he and Valerie shuddered. A scholastic career! The scholastic world! The *American* scholastic world! Shudder upon shudder! Give up their freedom, their full and beautiful life? Never! Never! Erasmus would be forty next birthday.

The "things" remained in warehouse. Valerie went to look at them. It cost her a dollar an hour, and horrid pangs. The "things," poor things, looked a bit shabby and wretched, in that warehouse.

However, New York was not all America. There was the great clean West. So the Melvilles went west, with Peter, but without the things. They tried living the simple life, in the mountains. But doing their own chores became almost a nightmare. "Things" are all very well to look at, but it's awful handling them, even when they're beautiful. To be the slave of hideous things, to keep a stove going, cook meals, wash dishes, carry water, and clean floors: pure horror of sordid anti-life!

In the cabin on the mountains, Valerie dreamed of Florence, the lost apartment; and her Bologna cupboard and Louis Quinze chairs, above all, her "Chartres" curtains, stood in New York—and costing fifty dollars a month.

A millionaire friend came to the rescue, offering them a cottage on the Californian coast—California! Where the new soul is to be born in man. With joy the idealists moved a little farther west, catching at new vine-props of hope.

And finding them straws! The millionaire cottage was perfectly equipped. It was perhaps as labour-savingly perfect as is possible: electric heating and

cooking, a white-and-pearl-enamelled kitchen, nothing
to make dirt except the human being himself. In an
hour or so the idealists had got through their chores.
They were "free"—free to hear the great Pacific
pounding the coast, and to feel a new soul filling their
bodies.

Alas! the Pacific pounded the coast with hideous
brutality, brute force itself! And the new soul, instead
of sweetly stealing into their bodies, seemed only
meanly to gnaw the old soul out of their bodies. To
feel you are under the fist of the most blind and
crunching brute force, to feel that your cherished
idealist's soul is being gnawed out of you, and only
irritation left in place of it: well, it isn't good enough.

After about nine months, the idealists departed from
the Californian west. It had been a great experience,
they were glad to have had it. But, in the long run, the
West was not the place for them, and they knew it.
No, the people who wanted new souls had better get
them. They, Valerie and Erasmus Melville, would like
to develop the old soul a little further. Anyway, they
had not felt any influx of new soul, on the Californian
coast. On the contrary.

So, with a slight hole in their material capital, they
returned to Massachusetts and paid a visit to Valerie's
parents, taking the boy along. The grandparents wel-
comed the child—poor expatriated boy—and were
rather cold to Valerie, but really cold to Erasmus.
Valerie's mother definitely said to Valerie, one day,

Things

that Erasmus ought to take a job, so that Valerie could live decently. Valerie haughtily reminded her mother of the beautiful apartment on the Arno, and the "wonderful" things in store in New York, and of the "marvellous and satisfying life" she and Erasmus had led. Valerie's mother said that she didn't think her daughter's life looked so very marvellous at present: homeless, with a husband idle at the age of forty, a child to educate, and a dwindling capital: looked the reverse of marvellous to *her*. Let Erasmus take some post in one of the universities.

"What post? What university?" interrupted Valerie.

"That could be found, considering your father's connexions and Erasmus's qualifications," replied Valerie's mother. "And you could get all your valuable things out of store, and have a really lovely home, which everybody in America would be proud to visit. As it is, your furniture is eating up your income, and you are living like rats in a hole, with nowhere to go to."

This was very true. Valerie was beginning to pine for a home, with her "things." Of course she could have sold her furniture for a substantial sum. But nothing would have induced her to. Whatever else passed away, religions, cultures, continents, and hopes, Valerie would *never* part from the "things" which she and Erasmus had collected with such passion. To these she was nailed.

But she and Erasmus still would not give up that

freedom, that full and beautiful life they had so believed in. Erasmus cursed America. He did not *want* to
earn a living. He panted for Europe.

Leaving the boy in charge of Valerie's parents, the
two idealists once more set off for Europe. In New
York they paid two dollars and looked for a brief, bitter hour at their "things." They sailed "student class"
—that is, third. Their income now was less than two
thousand dollars, instead of three. And they made
straight for Paris—cheap Paris.

They found Europe, this time, a complete failure.
"We have returned like dogs to our vomit," said
Erasmus; "but the vomit has staled in the meantime."
He found he couldn't stand Europe. It irritated every
nerve in his body. He hated America, too. But America
at least was a darn sight better than this miserable,
dirt-eating continent; which was by no means cheap
any more, either.

Valerie, with her heart on her things—she had really
burned to get them out of that warehouse, where they
had stood now for three years, eating up two thousand
dollars—wrote to her mother she thought Erasmus
would come back if he could get some suitable work in
America. Erasmus, in a state of frustration bordering
on rage and insanity, just went round Italy in a pov-
erty-stricken fashion, his coat-cuffs frayed, hating
everything with intensity. And when a post was found
for him in Cleveland University, to teach French,
Italian, and Spanish literature, his eyes grew more
beady, and his long, queer face grew sharper and more

rat-like, with utter baffled fury. He was forty, and the job was upon him.

"I think you'd better accept, dear. You don't care for Europe any longer. As you say, it's dead and finished. They offer us a house on the college campus, and mother says there's room in it for all our things. I think we'd better cable 'Accept.'"

He glowered at her like a cornered rat. One almost expected to see rat's whiskers twitching at the sides of the sharp nose.

"Shall I send the cablegram?" she asked.

"Send it!" he blurted.

And she went out and sent it.

He was a changed man, quieter, much less irritable. A load was off him. He was inside the cage.

But when he looked at the furnaces of Cleveland, vast and like the greatest of black forests, with red and white-hot cascades of gushing metal, and tiny gnomes of men, and terrific noises, gigantic, he said to Valerie:

"Say what you like, Valerie, this is the biggest thing the modern world has to show."

And when they were in their up-to-date little house on the campus of Cleveland University, and that woe-begone débris of Europe, Bologna cupboard, Venice bookshelves, Ravenna bishop's chair, Louis Quinze side-tables, "Chartres" curtains, Siena bronze lamps, all were arrayed, and all looked perfectly out of keeping, and therefore very impressive; and when the idealists had had a bunch of gaping people in, and Erasmus had showed off in his best European manner, but still

The Lovely Lady

quite cordial and American; and Valerie had been most
ladylike, but for all that, "we prefer America"; then
Erasmus said, looking at her with queer sharp eyes of
a rat:

"Europe's the mayonnaise all right, but America
supplies the good old lobster—what?"

"Every time!" she said, with satisfaction.

And he peered at her. He was in the cage, but it
was safe inside. And she, evidently, was her real self
at last. She had got the goods. Yet round his nose was
a queer, evil, scholastic look, of pure scepticism. But
he liked lobster.

The Overtone

His wife was talking to two other women. He lay on the lounge pretending to read. The lamps shed a golden light, and through the open door the night was lustrous, and a white moon went like a woman, unashamed and naked, across the sky. His wife, her dark hair tinged with grey looped low on her white neck, fingered as she talked the pearl that hung in a heavy, naked drop against the bosom of her dress. She was still a beautiful woman, and one who dressed like the night, for harmony. Her gown was of silk lace, all in flakes, as if the fallen, pressed petals of black and faded-red poppies were netted together with gossamer about her. She was fifty-one, and he was fifty-two. It seemed impossible. He felt his love cling round her like her dress, like a garment of dead leaves. She was talking to a quiet woman about the suffrage. The other girl, tall, rather aloof, sat listening in her chair, with the posture of one who neither accepts nor rejects, but who allows things to go on around her, and will know what she thinks only when she must act. She seemed to be looking away into the night. A scent of honeysuckle came through the open door. Then a large grey moth blundered into the light.

The Lovely Lady

It was very still, almost too silent, inside the room. Mrs. Renshaw's quiet, musical voice continued:

"But think of a case like Mrs. Mann's now. She is a clever woman. If she had slept in my cradle, and I in hers, she would have looked a greater lady than I do at this minute. But she married Mann, and she has seven children by him, and goes out charring. Her children she can never leave. So she must stay with a dirty, drunken brute like Mann. If she had an income of two pounds a week, she could say to him: 'Sir, good-bye to you,' and she would be well rid. But no, she is tied to him for ever."

They were discussing the State-endowment of mothers. She and Mrs. Hankin were bitterly keen upon it. Elsa Laskell sat and accepted their talk as she did the scent of the honeysuckle or the blundering adventure of the moth round the silk: it came burdened, not with the meaning of the words, but with the feeling of the woman's heart as she spoke. Perhaps she heard a nightingale in the park outside—perhaps she did. And then this talk inside drifted also to the girl's heart, like a sort of inarticulate music. Then she was vaguely aware of the man sprawled in his homespun suit upon the lounge. He had not changed for dinner: he was called unconventional.

She knew he was old enough to be her father, and yet he looked young enough to be her lover. They all seemed young, the beautiful hostess, too, but with a meaningless youth that cannot ripen, like an unfertilized flower which lasts a long time. He was a man she classed as a Dane—with fair, almost sandy hair, blue eyes, long loose limbs, and a boyish activity. But he was fifty-two—and he lay looking out on the night, with one of his hands swollen from hanging so long inert, silent. The women bored him.

Elsa Laskell sat in a sort of dreamy state, and the feelings of her hostess and the feeling of her host drifted like iridescence upon the quick of her soul, among the white touch of that moon out there, and the exotic heaviness of the honeysuckle, and the strange flapping of the moth. So still, it was, behind the murmur of talk: a silence of being. Of the third woman, Mrs. Hankin, the girl had no sensibility. But the night and the moon, the moth, Will Renshaw and Edith Renshaw and herself were all in full being, a harmony.

To him it was six months after his marriage, and the sky was the same, and the honeysuckle in the air. He was living again his crisis, as we all must, fretting and fretting against our failure, till we have worn away the thread of our life. It was six months after his marriage, and they were down at the little bungalow on the bank of the Soar. They were comparatively poor, though her father was rich, and his was well-to-do. And they were alone in the little two-roomed bungalow that stood on its wild bank over the river, among the honeysuckle bushes. He had cooked the evening meal, they had eaten the omelette and drunk the coffee, and all was settling into stillness.

He sat outside, by the remnants of the fire, looking at the country lying level and lustrous grey opposite him. Trees hung like vapour in a perfect calm under the moonlight. And that was the moon so perfectly naked and unfaltering, going her errand simply through the night. And that was the river faintly rustling. And there, down the darkness, he saw a flashing of activity white betwixt black twigs. It was the water mingling and thrilling with the moon. So! It made him quiver, and reminded him of the starlit rush of a hare. There was vividness then in all this lucid night, things flashing and quivering with being, almost as the soul quivers in the darkness of the eye. He could feel it. The night's great circle was the pupil of an eye, full of the mystery and the unknown fire of life, that does not burn away, but flickers unquenchable.

So he rose, and went to look for his wife. She sat with her dark head bent into the light of a reading-lamp, in the little hut. She wore a white dress, and he could see her shoulders' softness and curve through the lawn. Yet she did not look up when he moved. He stood in the doorway, knowing that she felt his presence. Yet she gave no sign.

"Will you come out?" he asked.

She looked up at him as if to find out what he wanted, and she was rather cold to him. But when he had repeated his request, she had risen slowly to acquiesce, and a tiny shiver had passed down her shoulders. So he unhung from its peg her beautiful Paisley shawl, with its tempered colours that looked as if they had faltered through the years and now were here in their essence, and put it round her. They sat again outside the little hut, under the moonlight. He held both her hands. They were heavy with rings. But one ring was his wedding ring. He had married her, and there was nothing more to own. He owned her, and the night was the pupil of her eye, in which was everything. He kissed her fingers, but she sat and made no sign. It was as he wished. He kissed her fingers again.

Then a corncrake began to call in the meadow across the river, a strange, dispassionate sound, that made him feel not quite satisfied, not quite sure. It was not all achieved. The moon, in her white and naked candour, was beyond him. He felt a little numbness, as one who has gloves on. He could not feel that clear, clean moon. There was something betwixt him and her, as if he had gloves on. Yet he ached for the clear touch, skin to skin—even of the moonlight. He wanted a further purity, a newer cleanness and nakedness. The corncrake cried, too. And he watched the moon, and he watched her light on his hands. It was like a butterfly on his glove, that he could see, but not feel. And he wanted to unglove himself. Quite clear, quite, quite bare to the moon, the touch of everything, he wanted to be. And after all, his wife was everything—moon, vapour of trees, trickling water, and drift of perfume—it was all his wife. The moon glistened on her finger-tips as he cherished them, and a flash came out of a diamond, among the darkness. So, even here in the quiet harmony, life was at a flash with itself.

"Come with me to the top of the red hill," he said to his wife quietly.

"But why?" she asked.

"Do come."

And dumbly she acquiesced, and her shawl hung gleaming above the white flash of her skirt. He wanted to hold her hand, but she was walking apart from him, in her long shawl. So he went to her side, humbly. And he was humble, but he felt it was great. He had looked into the whole of the night, as into the pupils of an eye. And now, he would come perfectly clear out of all his embarrassments of shame and darkness, clean as the moon who walked naked across the night, so that the whole night was as an effluence from her, the whole of it was hers, held in her effluence of moon-light, which was her perfect nakedness, uniting her to everything. Covering was barrier, like cloud across the moon.

The red hill was steep, but there was a tiny path from the bungalow, which he had worn himself. And in the effort of climbing, he felt he was struggling nearer and nearer to himself. Always he looked half round, where, just behind him, she followed, in the lustrous obscurity of her shawl. Her steps came with a little effort up the steep hill, and he loved her feet, he wanted to kiss them as they strove upwards in the gloom. He put aside the twigs and branches. There was a strong scent of honeysuckle like a thick strand of gossamer over his mouth.

He knew a place on the ledge of the hill, on the lip of the cliff, where the trees stood back and left a little dancing-green, high up above the water, there in the midst of miles of moonlit, lonely country. He parted the boughs, sure as a fox that runs to its lair. And they stood together on this little dancing-green presented towards the moon, with the red cliff cumbered with bushes going down to the river below, and the haze of moon-dust on the meadows, and the trees behind them, and only the moon could look straight into the place he had chosen.

She stood always a little way behind him. He saw her face all compounded of shadows and moonlight, and he dared not kiss her yet.

"Will you," he said, "will you take off your things and love me here?"

"I can't," she said.

He looked away to the moon. It was difficult to ask her again, yet it meant so much to him. There was not a sound in the night. He put his hand to his throat and began to unfasten his collar.

"Take off all your things and love me," he pleaded.

For a moment she was silent.

"I can't," she said.

Mechanically, he had taken off his flannel collar and pushed it into his pocket. Then he stood on the edge of the land, looking down into all that gleam, as into the living pupil of an eye. He was bareheaded to the moon. Not a breath of air ruffled his bare throat. Still, in the dropping folds of her shawl, she stood, a thing of dusk and moonlight, a little back. He ached with the earnestness of his desire. All he wanted was to give himself, clean and clear, into this night, this time. Of which she was all, she was everything. He could go to her now, under the white candour of the moon, without shame or shadow, but in his completeness loving her completeness, without a stain, without a shadow between them such as even a flower could cast. For this he yearned as never in his life he could yearn more deeply.

"Do take me," he said, gently parting the shawl on her breast. But she held it close, and her voice went hard.

"No—I can't," she said.

"Why?"

"I can't—let us go back."

He looked again over the countryside of dimness, saying in a low tone, his back towards her:

"But I love you—and I want you so much—like that, here and now. I'll never ask you anything again," he said quickly, passionately, as he turned to her. "Do this for me," he said. "I'll never trouble you for anything again. I promise."

"I can't," she said stubbornly, with some hopelessness in her voice.

"Yes," he said. "Yes. You trust me, don't you?"

"I don't want it. Not here—not now," she said.

"Do," he said. "Yes."

"You can have me in the bungalow. Why do you want me here?" she asked.

"But I do. Have me, Edith. Have me now."

"No," she said, turning away. "I want to go down."

"And you won't?"

172

The Overtone

"No—I can't."

There was something like fear in her voice. They went down the hill together. And he did not know how he hated her, as if she had kept him out of the promised land that was justly his. He thought he was too generous to bear her a grudge. So he had always held himself deferential to her. And later that evening he had loved her. But she hated it, it had been really his hate ravaging her. Why had he lied, calling it love? Ever since, it had seemed the same, more or less. So that he had ceased to come to her, gradually. For one night she had said: "I think a man's body is ugly—all in parts with mechanical joints." And now he had scarcely had her for some years. For she thought him an ugliness. And there were no children.

Now that everything was essentially over, for both of them, they lived on the surface, and had good times. He drove to all kinds of unexpected places in his motor car, bathed where he liked, said what he liked, and did what he liked. But nobody minded very much his often aggressive unconventionality. It was only fencing with the foils. There was no danger in his thrusts. He was a castrated bear. So he prided himself on being a bear, on being known as an uncouth bear.

It was not often he lay and let himself drift. But always when he did, he held it against her that on the night when they climbed the red bank, she refused to have him. There were perhaps many things he might have held against her, but this was the only one that remained: his real charge against her on the Judgment

Day. Why had she done it? It had been, he might almost say, a holy desire on his part. It had been almost like taking off his shoes before God. Yet she refused him, she who was his religion to him. Perhaps she had been afraid, she who was so good—afraid of the big righteousness of it—as if she could not trust herself so near the Burning Bush, dared not go near for transfiguration, afraid of herself.

It was a thought he could not bear. Rising softly, because she was still talking, he went out into the night.

Elsa Laskell stirred uneasily in her chair. Mrs. Renshaw went on talking like a somnambule, not because she really had anything to say about the State-endowment of mothers, but because she had a weight on her heart that she wanted to talk away. The girl heard, and lifted her hand, and stirred her fingers uneasily in the dark purple porphyry bowl, where pink rose-leaves and crimson, thrown this morning from the stem, lay gently shrivelling. There came a slight acrid scent of new rose-petals. And still the girl lifted her long white fingers among the red and pink in the dark bowl, as if they stirred in blood.

And she felt the nights behind like a purple bowl into which the woman's heart-beats were shed, like rose-leaves fallen and left to wither and go brown. For Mrs. Renshaw had waited for him. During happy days of stillness and blueness she had moved, while the sunshine glancing through her blood made flowers in her

174

heart, like blossoms underground thrilling with expectancy, lovely fragrant things that would have delighted to appear. And all day long she had gone secretly and quietly saying, saying: "Tonight—tonight they will blossom for him. Tonight I shall be a bed of blossom for him, all narcissi and fresh fragrant things shaking for joy, when he comes with his deeper sunshine, when he turns the darkness like mould, and brings them forth with his sunshine for spade. Yea, there are two suns; him in the sky and that other, warmer one whose beams are our radiant bodies. He is a sun to me, shining full on my heart when he comes, and everything stirs." But he had come like a bitter morning. He had never bared the sun of himself to her—a sullen day he had been on her heart, covered with cloud impenetrable. She had waited so heavy anxious, with such a wealth of possibility. And he in his blindness had never known. He could never let the real rays of his love through the cloud of fear, and mistrust. For once she had denied him. And all her flowers had been shed inwards, so that her heart was like a heap of leaves, brown, withered, almost scentless petals that had never given joy to anyone. And yet again she had come to him pregnant with beauty and love, but he had been afraid. When she lifted her eyes to him, he had looked aside. The kisses she needed like warm raindrops he dared not give, till she was parched and gone hard, and did not want them. Then he gave kisses enough. But he never trusted himself. When she was open and eager to him, he was afraid. When she was shut, it was like playing at pride, to pull her petals apart, a game that gave him pleasure.

So they had been mutually afraid of each other, but he most often. Whenever she had needed him at some mystery of love, he had overturned her censers and her sacraments, and made profane love in her sacred place. Which was why, at last, she had hated his body; but perhaps she had hated it at first, or feared it so much, that it was hate.

And he had said to her: "If *we* don't have children, you might have them by another man—" which was surely one of the cruellest things a woman ever heard from her husband. For so little was she his, that he would give her a caller and not mind. This was all the wife she was to him. He was a free and easy man, and brought home to dinner any man who pleased him, from a beggar upwards. And his wife was to be as public as his board.

Nay, to the very bowl of her heart, any man might put his lips and he would not mind. And so, she sadly set down the bowl from between her two hands of offering, and went always empty, and aloof.

Yet they were married, they were good friends. It was said they were the most friendly married couple in the county. And this was it. And all the while, like a scent, the bitter psalm of the woman filled the room.

"Like a garden in winter, I was full of bulbs and roots, I was full of little flowers, all conceived inside me.

The Overtone

"And they were all shed away unborn, little abortions of flowers.

"Every day I went like a bee gathering honey from the sky and among the stars I rummaged for yellow honey, filling it in my comb.

"Then I broke the comb, and put it to your lips. But you turned your mouth aside, and said, 'You have made my face unclean, and smeared my mouth.'

"And week after week my body was a vineyard, my veins were vines. And as the grapes, the purple drops grew full and sweet, I crushed them in a bowl, I treasured the wine.

"Then when the bowl was full I came with joy to you. But you in fear started away, and the bowl was thrown from my hands, and broke in pieces at my feet.

"Many times, and many times, I said, 'The hour is striking,' but he answered, 'Not yet.'

"Many times and many times he has heard the cock-crow, and gone out and wept, he knew not why.

"I was a garden and he ran in me as in the grass.

"I was a stream, and he threw his waste in me.

"I held the rainbow balanced on my outspread hands, and he said, 'You open your hands and give me nothing.'

"What am I now but a bowl of withered leaves, but a kaleidoscope of broken beauties, but an empty bee-hive, yea, a rich garment rusted that no one has worn, a dumb singer, with the voice of a nightingale yet making discord.

"And it was over with me, and my hour is gone.

The Lovely Lady

And soon like a barren sea-shell on the strand, I shall be crushed underfoot to dust.

"But meanwhile I sing to those that listen with their ear against me, of the sea that gave me form and being, the everlasting sea, and in my song is nothing but bitterness, for of the fluid life of the sea I have no more, but I am to be dust, that powdery stuff the sea knows not. I am to be dead, who was born of life, silent who was made a mouth, formless who was all of beauty. Yea, I was a seed that held the heavens lapped up in bud, with a whirl of stars and a steady moon.

"And the seed is crushed that never sprouted, there is a heaven lost, and stars and a moon that never came forth.

"I was a bud that never was discovered, and in my shut chalice, skies and lake water and brooks lie crumbling, and stars and the sun are smeared out, and birds are a little powdery dust, and their singing is dry air, and I am a dark chalice."

And the girl, hearing the hostess talk, still talk, and yet her voice like the sound of a sea-shell whispering hoarsely of despair, rose and went out into the garden, timidly, beginning to cry. For what should she do for herself?

Renshaw, leaning on the wicket that led to the paddock, called:

"Come on, don't be alarmed—Pan is dead."

And then she bit back her tears. For when he said, "Pan is dead," he meant Pan was dead in his own long, loose Dane's body. Yet she was a nymph still, and, if Pan were dead, she ought to die. So with tears she went up to him.

"It's all right out here," he said. "By Jove, when you see a night like this, how can you say that life's a tragedy—or death either, for that matter?"

"What is it, then?" she asked.

"Nay, that's one too many—a joke, eh?"

"I think," she said, "one has no business to be irreverent."

"Who?" he asked.

"You," she said, "and me, and all of us."

Then he leaned on the wicket, thinking till he laughed.

"Life's a real good thing," he said.

"But why protest it?" she answered.

And again he was silent.

"If the moon came nearer and nearer," she said, "and were a naked woman, what would you do?"

"Fetch a wrap, probably," he said.

"Yes—you would do that," she answered.

"And if he were a man, ditto?" he teased.

"If a star came nearer and were a naked man, I should look at him."

"That is surely very improper," he mocked, with still a tinge of yearning.

"If he were a star come near . . ." she answered.

Again he was silent.

"You are a queer fish of a girl," he said.

The Lovely Lady

They stood at the gate, facing the silver-grey paddock. Presently their hostess came out, a long shawl hanging from her shoulders.

"So you are here," she said. "Were you bored?"

"I was," he replied amiably. "But there, you know I always am."

"And I forgot," replied the girl.

"What were you talking about?" asked Mrs. Renshaw, simply curious. She was not afraid of her husband's running loose.

"We were just saying, 'Pan is dead,' " said the girl.

"Isn't that rather trite?" asked the hostess.

"Some of us miss him fearfully," said the girl.

"For what reason?" asked Mrs. Renshaw.

"Those of us who are nymphs—just lost nymphs among farmlands and suburbs. I wish Pan were alive."

"Did he die of old age?" mocked the hostess.

"Don't they say, when Christ was born, a voice was heard in the air saying, 'Pan is dead.' I wish Christ needn't have killed Pan."

"I wonder how He managed it," said Renshaw.

"By disapproving of him, I suppose," replied his wife. And her retort cut herself, and gave her a sort of fakir pleasure.

"The men are all women now," she said, "since the fauns died in a frost one night."

"A frost of disapproval," said the girl.

"A frost of fear," said Renshaw.

There was a silence.

"Why was Christ afraid of Pan?" said the girl suddenly.

"Why was Pan so much afraid of Christ, that he died?" asked Mrs. Renshaw bitterly.

"And all his fauns in a frost one night," mocked Renshaw. Then a light dawned on him. "Christ was woman, and Pan was man," he said. It gave him real joy to say this, bitterly, keenly—a thrust into himself, and into his wife. "But the fauns and satyrs are there —you have only to remove the surplices that all men wear nowadays."

"Nay," said Mrs. Renshaw, "it is not true—the surplices have grown into their limbs, like Hercules' garment."

"That his wife put on him," said Renshaw.

"Because she was afraid of him—not because she loved him," said the girl.

"She imagined that all her lovely wasted hours wove him a robe of love," said Mrs. Renshaw. "It was to her horror she was mistaken. You can't weave love out of waste."

"When I meet a man," said the girl, "I shall look down the pupil of his eye, for a faun. And after a while it will come, skipping . . ."

"Perhaps a satyr," said Mrs. Renshaw bitterly.

"No," said the girl, "because satyrs are old, and I have seen some fearfully young men."

"Will is young even now—quite a boy," said his wife.

"Oh, no!" cried the girl. "He says that neither life nor death is a tragedy. Only somebody very old could say that."

There was a tension in the night. The man felt something give way inside him.

"Yes, Edith," he said, with a quiet, bitter joy of cruelty, "I am old."

The wife was frightened.

"You are always preposterous," she said quickly, crying inside herself. She knew she herself had been never young.

"I shall look in the eyes of my man for the faun," the girl continued in a sing-song, "and I shall find him. Then I shall pretend to run away from him. And both our surplices, and all the crucifix, will be outside the wood. Inside nymph and faun, Pan and his satyrs, ah, yes: for Christ and the Cross is only for daytime, and bargaining. Christ came to make us deal honourably.

"But love is no deal, nor merchant's bargaining, and Christ neither spoke of it nor forbade it. He was afraid of it. If once His faun, the faun of the young Jesus had run free, seen one white nymph's brief breast, He would not have been content to die on a Cross—and then the men would have gone on cheating the women in life's business, all the time. Christ made one bargain in mankind's business—and He made it for the women's sake—I suppose for His mother's, since He was fatherless. And Christ made a bargain for me, and I shall avail myself of it. I won't be cheated by my man. When between my still hands I weave silk out of the

182

air, like a cocoon, he shall not take it to pelt me with. He shall draw it forth and weave it up. For I want to finger the sunshine I have drawn through my body, stroke it, and have joy of the fabric.

"And when I run wild on the hills with Dionysus, and shall come home like a bee that has rolled in floury crocuses, he must see the wonder on me, and make bread of it.

"And when I say to him, 'It is harvest in my soul,' he shall look in my eyes and lower his nets where the shoal moves in a throng in the dark, and lift out the living blue silver for me to see, and know, and taste.

"All this, my faun in commerce, my faun at traffic with me.

"And if he cheat me, he must take his chance.

"But I will not cheat him, in his hour, when he runs like a faun after me. I shall flee, but only to be over-taken. I shall flee, but never out of the wood to the crucifix. For that is to deny I am a nymph; since how can a nymph cling at the crucifix? Nay, the cross is the sign I have on my money, for honesty.

"In the morning, when we come out of the wood, I shall say to him: 'Touch the cross, and prove you will deal fairly,' and if he will not, I will set the dogs of anger and judgment on him, and they shall chase him. But if, perchance, some night he contrive to crawl back into the wood, beyond the crucifix, he will be faun and I nymph, and I shall have no knowledge what happened outside, in the realm of the crucifix. But in the morning, I shall say: 'Touch the cross, and prove you will deal fairly.' And being renewed, he will touch the cross.

"Many a dead faun I have seen, like dead rabbits poisoned lying about the paths, and many a dead nymph, like swans that could not fly and the dogs destroyed.

"But I am a nymph and a woman, and Pan is for me, and Christ is for me.

"For Christ I cover myself in my robe, and weep, and vow my vow of honesty.

"For Pan I throw my coverings down and run headlong through the leaves, because of the joy of running.

"And Pan will give me my children and joy, and Christ will give me my pride.

"And Pan will give me my man, and Christ my husband.

"To Pan I am nymph, to Christ I am woman.

"And Pan is in the darkness, and Christ in the pale light.

"And night shall never be day, and day shall never be night.

"But side by side they shall go, day and night, night and day, for ever apart, for ever together.

"Pan and Christ, Christ and Pan.

"Both moving over me, so when in the sunshine I go in my robes among my neighbours, I am a Christian. But when I run robeless through the dark-scented woods alone, I am Pan's nymph.

"Now I must go, for I want to run away. Not run away from myself, but to myself.

184

The Overtone

"For neither am I a lamp that stands in the way in the sunshine.

"Now am I a sundial foolish at night.

"I am myself, running through light and shadow for ever, a nymph and a Christian; I, not two things, but an apple with a gold side and a red, a freckled deer, a stream that tinkles and a pool where light is drowned; I, no fragment, no half-thing like the day, but a black-bird with a white breast and underwings, a peewit, a wild thing, beyond understanding."

"I wonder if we shall hear the nightingale tonight," said Mrs. Renshaw.

"He's a gurgling fowl—I'd rather hear a linnet," said Renshaw. "Come a drive with me tomorrow, Miss Laskell."

And the three went walking back to the house. And Elsa Laskell was glad to get away from them.